Mary's L

My dear,

Hope you will enjoy
reading this story to your
beautiful Grandchildren.
  Merry Christmas
      Love,
        Maryann

Gunhild Sehlin

Mary's Little Donkey
and the Flight to Egypt

Floris Books

Translated by Hugh Latham and Donald Maclean
Illustrated by Jan Verheijn

Originally published in Swedish under the title
Marias lilla åsna in 1962 and *Åsnan och barnet* in 1964.
Mary's Little Donkey first published in English
in 1979 by Floris Books.
Mary's Little Donkey and the Flight to Egypt first
published in English in 1987 by Floris Books
Reprinted in 1990.

British Library CIP Data available

ISBN 0-86315-064-0

Printed in Great Britain
by Dotesios Ltd, Trowbridge, Wilts.

Contents

The laziest donkey in all Nazareth

Long, long ago a little donkey lived in Nazareth, in the Holy Land. He was quite different from all the other donkeys in the town. He was as lazy and unkempt and dirty as they were clean and hard-working. All the same he moved very beautifully and he held his head the highest of them all.

Sometimes all the donkeys rambled along in a long line carrying firewood from the little wood right into Nazareth. They all trotted along eagerly. They always tried to see who could carry most home to his master. Right at the end of the line the lazy donkey shambled along and whenever he had a chance of shaking off a few branches, that's just what he did. Sometimes he tried to push past one or two of his comrades, for he did not like being last. But the others always lashed out at him and stopped him, saying, "Stay where you belong, you lazy donkey, you!"

In the evening when all the donkeys came home to their stalls they were combed and brushed until their coats shone like silk. Now the lazy donkey belonged to the richest man in Nazareth, but he had absolutely the laziest groom to look after him. This man never combed him and that is why the donkey always ran around dirty and matted. It annoyed the other donkeys that he held his head so proudly all the same.

"Aren't you ashamed then?" they said, "Fancy stretching your neck and strutting around when you are so dirty."

And the oldest and wisest donkey said, "Don't you

really understand? It just isn't right. You can't give yourself airs and look as dirty as you do."

But the lazy donkey was not troubled a bit by all this. "I'll show them one day," he thought.

Of course he didn't really know what it was he was going to show them, only that it would be something wonderfully beautiful and strange.

The people of the little town often laughed at the lazy donkey. "He must watch it, or he'll starve one day," they said, "He's almost too lazy to eat."

Even his master sighed sometimes: "He looks really terrible. Simon, get on with it now and comb him thoroughly."

"Yes, master," answered Simon.

But as soon as his master had gone, Simon hung the brush on its nail and lay in the grass. And so sometimes the little donkey was only half combed. Then the people and the animals laughed and mocked him even more.

"Just wait!" the little donkey thought to himself, "I'll show you all one day." But he didn't say anything.

From time to time Simon had to fetch water from the town well. He didn't like doing this at all, as he thought it was work for a woman; but he had to obey when his master gave the order. He threw two leather water buckets over the donkey's back and the pair set off. If the groom felt that they were going too slowly he drove the donkey on with a stick. But that didn't happen very often, for Simon was lazy too and was seldom in a hurry.

Early in the morning it was always lively and busy at the well, for all the women were fetching water in large, earthenware pitchers. They filled their pitchers up to the brim with clear, fresh water and carried them home on their heads. The women were very skilful, and not one of them spilt a single drop of the precious water and no one dropped a pitcher. Often the women

8

sat for a little while by the well and gossiped before returning home, but not for long, for they wanted to get back while the morning was still fresh and cool.

One morning a young woman, whose name was Mary, met Simon and his donkey. She was on the way home with her pitcher of water. Mary looked at the little donkey and said: "What a beautiful donkey! It's a thousand pities that he's so dirty."

She stopped for a minute and stroked the donkey behind his ears. Oh, how lovely that was! He couldn't remember ever having been stroked before. And on the way home he was thinking so much about Mary that he didn't notice when Simon shouted and hit and thumped him.

From that day on the lazy donkey often saw Mary at the same time at the fountain. And every time she had time for a friendly word for the little animal and she stroked him.

When the donkey went tripping along home after this his bearing was even prouder and he held his head even higher than usual. All his comrades grumbled about this. They said: "Just what's the matter with him now? Every day he makes himself out to be more important, and at the same time he gets lazier and lazier. It's disgraceful!"

But the little donkey took no notice at all of what his comrades said.

"If they only knew!" he thought to himself.

Every morning now the donkey pricked up his ears and tried to hear if Simon was being sent by his master to the well. If the groom came along with the water buckets he was so delighted and happy that he could hardly keep still while they were being fastened. Then he set off to the well at such a pace, uphill and downhill, that the astonished Simon could scarcely keep up.

If Mary wasn't there the donkey thought that she

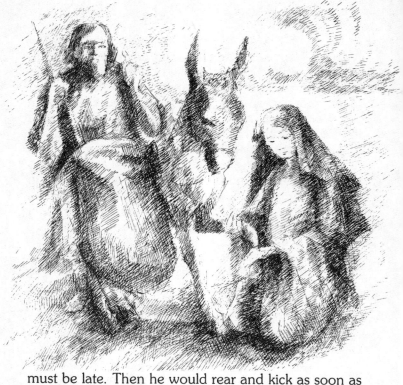

must be late. Then he would rear and kick as soon as Simon wanted to fasten the water containers on, and so it would be some time before they were ready to set out for home. Even then he would straddle his legs and refuse to budge and get himself whipped and beaten, keeping it up until Mary came and stroked him and spoke some friendly words to him.

After that he trotted home and carried his head high.

"He is quite mad," Simon said to the other grooms when he came home.

One day the donkey had trodden a sharp piece of stone into his foot. This made every step he took terribly painful and made him limp.

10

"That's his punishment," the other donkeys said. "It serves him right. Now let him try to go on playing the fool."

Mary noticed it next morning. She asked, "What's wrong with the donkey's foot? Has he hurt himself?"

"I don't think so," Simon answered, who hadn't even noticed that the donkey was limping.

"It's a shame not to help the poor animal," Mary said angrily.

"There's nothing wrong with him," replied Simon. "He's just lazy and vicious."

"Can I just have a look at your foot?" Mary asked the donkey.

"Look out, he'll kick," warned Simon. "It's dangerous to touch his hoofs."

"He'll let me," Mary said.

Willingly the donkey lifted his foot and kept quite still. Mary found the sharp piece of stone and pulled it out.

"So that was the trouble," Mary said. "Now you can go on trotting about so beautifully and upright."

When the donkey came home his comrades were all angry because he could walk and run quite well again. They grumbled terribly. But it didn't trouble the lazy donkey one little bit.

"If only they knew!" he thought. "Oh, if only they knew!"

The sale of the donkey

With her pitcher of water on her head Mary strolled home. She had to go a long way through the narrow, winding alleys. She was quite exhausted when at last she reached her house. She put the pitcher down, sat down on a bench in her garden and rested.

Then Joseph, her husband, came out from his workshop. He always took great care of Mary, and when he saw how tired she was he was worried.

"If I could only buy you a donkey," he sighed. "He could carry the water and firewood for you, and you wouldn't have to drag such weights along."

"That would be wonderful," said Mary. "How I would love to have a donkey. But we both know that we can't afford to buy one. Don't worry, Joseph. When I have had a bit of rest I can carry on. God gives me the strength. Just wait, and you'll see."

So Joseph went back into his workshop. He had to work from dawn to dusk to make enough money for his family's needs. That's why he was so sad that he hadn't enough money to buy a donkey.

As he stood there and planed the wood an idea came to him. "If I were to get up an hour earlier every day and were to work faster than I have done until now, I might be able to earn enough extra money to pay for a donkey," he said to himself. "I must try to do it. Mary looked so tired today."

From this day on Joseph got up before it was light and worked as hard as he could. Fortunately he had enough orders. Slowly but surely his savings grew bigger.

"Dear Joseph," Mary said many times, "you are working too hard. We have money for all we need."

"I like to work," was Joseph's answer to that.

"It's too much for your strength," said Mary anxiously.

"Certainly not," replied Joseph and smiled mysteriously.

He did not tell Mary that he was saving up to buy her a donkey. That was to be a surprise.

One day Joseph realized that Mary was an unusually long time coming back from the fountain. Although he still had a lot of work to do, he shook the wood shavings from his coat and went out into the street. As soon as he caught sight of Mary he hurried towards her. She was sitting utterly exhausted at the side of the road. The pitcher stood on the ground by her side.

"Dear Joseph," said Mary, "I was just going to have a bit of a rest and then I can go on carrying the water. You need not trouble yourself."

But Joseph lifted the pitcher and carried it in his arms — he couldn't carry it on his head like the women. How exhausting it was to carry the water! Mary followed him.

That night he took his money out and counted it. "I must buy a donkey at once," he thought, but he said nothing to Mary.

Joseph went to the richest man in Nazareth. Anyone who owned so many donkeys could surely spare one of them.

"Will you sell me a donkey?" Joseph asked the rich man.

"Can you afford the price? A good animal costs a lot of money."

"Yes, sir," Joseph said with some hesitation. "How much do you want?"

But the rich man wanted much, much more money

than Joseph had. He would have to work for many more months before he could earn so much money.

"Come again, when you are able to pay," said the rich man.

"But I must have one now. Mary is not strong and cannot carry everything herself. Couldn't I pay the balance later?"

"No," said the rich man. "I must have all the money now."

Joseph just went on standing there looking rather miserable and confused. But the rich man acted as though he were in a hurry.

"Good-bye," he said. "Come again when you are able to pay. Then we can do business."

And he turned to go. But Joseph held him firmly by his coat.

"Sir, have you not just one donkey that is cheaper than the others?"

"No," said the rich man. "I have only the finest animals."

Just then, though, he remembered the lazy, dirty donkey everyone laughed at. He would gladly get rid of that one. He certainly was a disgrace to the whole stable. All right, let this working man have that one for his money.

"Just a moment", he said. "I do have one you could buy."

He called Simon and ordered him to bring the lazy donkey out.

Joseph waited eagerly. But when Simon arrived with the donkey he saw straightaway that this was not a good and reliable animal. It was the only one, though, that he could afford.

And so the rich man took the money and Joseph took the donkey.

Then Joseph set out with the donkey on the long road home.

14

But the donkey thought that he had done enough work for that day and he had no desire at all to go on running about. He could not understand either why or where this strange man was taking him. So he resisted with all his strength.

In some places the path went up steps. When at last Joseph and the donkey reached the top the donkey suddenly pulled back and made Joseph let go of the reins. Then the donkey let himself slide back down again, looking, as he did so, as if he were laughing. He often played Simon up by trying to do this, and the drover lost his temper whenever he managed it. But Joseph did not get angry. He only sighed and spoke gently to him. "Just try to walk properly for once, or we shan't get home before dark."

And Joseph had to pull the obstinate creature up the steps again. "I am afraid Mary will have more trouble than help with this beast," he thought sadly as he wiped the sweat from his brow.

At last they reached home. Joseph tied the donkey to an olive tree in front of the house and went in.

"I've bought a donkey for you, Mary," he said, but his voice sounded rather downcast.

"O Joseph," cried Mary, "how good of you. Is that why you have been working so hard?"

"I wanted to get you a really good, hard-working donkey who would give you a lot of help. But I had only enough money for the laziest, dirtiest beast that ever trotted about on God's earth."

"Did you say lazy?" Mary asked eagerly. "You surely can't mean the donkey at the well. Does he move more beautifully than all the other donkeys, and does he hold his head higher than the others do? And is he terribly dirty?"

"Yes, he's dirty all right," Joseph said sadly. "I did not notice if he moves beautifully. He's more inclined to sit on his backside and get himself pulled along."

But Mary was already outside. "O Joseph! It is him! Ever since you spoke to me about a donkey this is just the one I've always wanted to have. But I never believed that my wish would come true. Thank you, thank you, dear, dear Joseph."

"But Mary," said the astonished Joseph, "why do you want just the laziest, stupidest and dirtiest donkey in all Nazareth?"

"I'll tell you why," said Mary, who had already fetched a brush and started to groom the donkey. "Because he can become a splendid and very special donkey. Haven't you noticed what intelligent eyes he has? A donkey who walks so freely and lightly can certainly learn to carry a heavy load. Anyone who carries his head so high is surely noble and clean. It wasn't his fault that nobody groomed him. I am so pleased with my donkey, Joseph. How can I ever thank you?"

"Perhaps you are right," Joseph said thoughtfully. "And I am so pleased that you are happy. But let me groom him."

And Joseph groomed the donkey until he really shone. Mary stood at his side and gently patted him.

But the donkey was now utterly confused. What could all this mean? Why was he here with Mary? Anyway, he made up his mind to stay as long as possible. They would only get him away if they carried him.

When Mary took the reins and said, "Come along!" he followed her willingly.

"This is where you are to sleep," Mary said.

She fetched him an armful of sweet-smelling hay and put it in his manger. "Now eat and have a good sleep," she said and patted him. "Here is a new comrade for you," she explained to the sheep and goats in the stable. "Be good to him."

Then Mary left. The donkey tried to break away.

16

"Baah," bleated the sheep. "Welcome. It's good to have a new comrade. And a donkey was just what Mary badly needed."

"Maah", bleated the goats. "Welcome! You understand that you are going to help Mary, don't you? We've been waiting a long time for you. It's good that you are here now."

This calmed the little donkey down. He was very surprised, for other animals had never been friendly to him.

"What kind of stable is this?" he asked.

"It's Mary's, it's Mary's," cried all the lambs and the baby goats. "It's the best house in all the world. Where do you come from then?"

The little donkey didn't answer. He just marvelled at it all.

"I'll never go away from here," he decided.

All round him the sheep and goats were sleeping now and soon the little donkey fell asleep too. But even in his deepest dream he went on thinking, "No, I'll never go away from here, never . . ."

The great mystery

The little donkey woke early next morning. "What a happy dream I had in the night," he thought. "A strange man came and took me to Mary, whom I like so much. And the man said that I belong to Mary. And she was delighted, for she likes me too. I was brushed and combed until I was as lovely as the day. Ah well, what a dream that was, what a marvellous dream. It's strange though — I'm still clean and tidy. It's very pleasant, too, just like it was in the dream."

The little donkey cried "Hee-haw", which sounded as though he was trying to laugh.

It woke up the sheep and goats in Joseph's stable. "Good morning, little donkey," they said. "We hope you had a beautiful dream last night."

"Oh, indeed I did," the little donkey answered. "I had the most beautiful dream there is in the whole world."

"I'm so glad," said the oldest sheep politely. "Look, Mary's coming now."

All the animals jostled and pushed in their stalls trying to be the first to greet Mary. What a bleating there was!

"Mary?" pondered the donkey looking all round him. "I really am with Mary. That wasn't a dream at all. *It was true!*"

Quietly and patiently he stood and waited until Mary had stroked all the animals and given them something to eat. Last of all she came to the little donkey's stall.

"Good morning, my little donkey. Now you must eat well, so that you can grow big and strong. When

I have milked the goats and taken them and the sheep
to the meadow we two must fetch water from the well.
Until then just go on munching your hay.''

But the little donkey was so overjoyed that he forgot
to eat. Joseph came and looked at him too.

"He really does look handsome now," he
marvelled. "You really can scarcely recognize him."

"Dear Joseph, he is the most beautiful donkey there
is," said Mary.

"But I'm afraid you will have a lot of trouble with
him when you fetch the water. You just don't know
how stubborn he is."

"If you will just make him a yoke that fits well and

19

doesn't rub, I'll fasten the water buckets to it and you'll soon see how good he is," Mary answered.

Joseph made what she wanted straight away. He measured the donkey and went into the workshop. You could hear him working away busily with axe and plane. Then out he came carrying a yoke that fitted the donkey's back.

"It rubs just a little on the right side. I can correct that," he said and vanished again into his workshop. He came out with the yoke just as Mary finished her morning work. When they both placed it on the donkey's back it fitted exactly.

"Dear Joseph," Mary said gratefully, "no one can make as good a yoke as you."

The little donkey found out that Mary was right. He had never had a yoke before that did not chafe him and hurt him. This one was smooth and steady and comfortable.

Joseph fastened the water buckets to it.

"Good-bye, Joseph, we are going now," cried Mary, smiling happily.

"Good-bye," sighed Joseph. "I only hope you can manage the donkey. I am very worried."

"There is no need to be," laughed Mary. "We shall get along all right. Just look how daintily he trips along." Joseph shook his head as he went back to his workshop.

Mary was proud and happy as she walked along through the narrow, winding streets of Nazareth with her little donkey. She passed many low, square houses with flat roofs, and women and girls were coming out of every house carrying water pitchers on their heads.

Mary went in front, with the donkey behind her. She just could not imagine that the donkey would be difficult and she didn't lead him at all. She had placed the reins over the yoke, and the donkey followed her like a good, obedient dog. Not once did he do anything wrong. How could anyone misbehave with Mary? When they reached the well the women and the girls flocked round the little donkey.

"But Mary!" they said, "What a beautiful donkey. Where have you managed to borrow him? He doesn't belong to you, does he?"

"Yes he does. He belongs to me," Mary answered proudly. "Joseph bought him for me."

"Joseph?" they asked in surprise. "A beautiful animal like this? It must have been very expensive."

Mary just laughed. The girls stroked the donkey and praised his appearance. The most beautiful of them plucked red flowers and fastened them to his forehead.

"Look, Mary, now he could belong to a queen," this girl said. "I have never seen a donkey who carries his head so proudly."

Mary filled the water buckets and fastened them to the yoke.

"Let's go home," she said. "But take care that no water slops out."

And the donkey went carefully and precisely step by step, choosing the best place for his hoofs so that none of the fresh water would spill.

Joseph had all the time kept looking for Mary and the donkey and he hurried out of his workshop as soon as they reached home.

"How did it go?" he asked. "Why are you back so soon? Was he so much trouble that you had to turn back? Just sit down, Mary, and have a rest. I'll go. I'll soon deal with him."

"Joseph dear," Mary replied, "he is the best donkey in all the world. I told you so before. We have been to the well. Look! The water is up to the brim and not a drop has been spilt."

Joseph was then lost in wonder. He gazed for some while at the water and then said: "All creatures are docile and gentle as lambs when you deal with them, because you are so good."

"I'm not good," Mary said, "but the little donkey is, and so are you, Joseph dear."

Mary led the donkey then out to the meadow, where the other animals were grazing.

"Thank you for helping me," Mary said. "Now have a good rest, my own little donkey. You don't need to work any more today, but soon it will be harvest time and believe me, there'll be a lot to do then."

The meadow was not large but it was fine for the animals. A little stream flowed down from the mountains and along its banks grew green grass and tasty herbs. The air was full of a pleasant fragrance and a gnarled old olive tree gave shade when the sun's heat was strongest.

Today the animals told the little donkey a secret.

First of all they asked him if he wanted to hear the great secret.

Yes, of course he wanted to hear it.

Then they asked him if he could really keep the great secret to himself.

"Yes," he said, "I believe I can."

So they told him to listen. The oldest sheep drew a deep breath and began to speak. The donkey quivered with curiosity. But the younger sheep and the little goats, who knew already what was coming, grew so excited at the thought of the secret that they couldn't keep still. They started to jump, and to dance and to bleat. The large animals tried to calm them down but it was a long time before it was quiet enough at last for the oldest sheep to begin.

She took a deep breath, and opened her mouth . . . but she was soon drowned by a whole flock of chirping and twittering birds. All the birds of Nazareth came flying there and they settled in the large olive-tree. They had heard the din made by the young sheep and the little goats and realized at once that it was something to do with the great secret. They wanted to be there too. Even though they knew about it already they had to sing wholeheartedly for joy whenever they thought about it. The old sheep had to wait until they were quiet. The poor donkey, though, had meanwhile almost fainted with curiosity.

At last the sheep was able to speak. For the third time she took a deep breath and said, "baa . . ."

But then the happy little grasshoppers began to chirp. In that country they are called cicadas and they too lived round the olive-tree. This shrill chirping was a deafening sound to the donkey. But the cicadas thought it made a very pretty sound, and besides, it was their nature to be happy.

When at last they stopped, the old sheep took a deep breath for the fourth time. She really wanted to speak of the secret solemnly and quietly, just as a secret really should be told, but instead she blurted it out very loud: "Mary is going to have a child, a son!"

At that she was interrupted again. The little sheep and goats gambolled and danced, the birds started to sing a new song and the grasshoppers chirped. The donkey, though, gave such a loud cry of joy that even the grasshoppers couldn't be heard any more.

It was a long time before the animals quietened down again.

Then it became very still. They were all thinking of Mary's child who was soon to come into the world. Yes, now it was so silent that you could hear the gentle murmur of the stream.

The little sheep had suddenly become quiet. They stood there pondering what games they could play with the child. Perhaps he would like to play hide-and-seek round the old olive-tree. The little goats were wondering if he would like to run races with them. The cicadas decided to teach the child how to chirp. The birds were composing lovely cradle songs. They knew that a little human child can't play and romp straight away, but has to sleep a lot in order to grow and thrive.

Of course the grown-up animals understood that all right. The goats knew that the child needed good milk, and they were considering which plants they ought to eat to make their milk more nourishing than usual. They wanted to avoid bitter herbs and grasses so that their milk wouldn't be sour.

The sheep for their part reckoned that the little one would need soft, warm clothing and they were wondering if their wool would be delicate enough if they were careful and didn't let it get dirty.

But the little donkey had a wonderful idea. The small son of the rich man had a donkey with a saddle to ride. It always looked very smart when the boy came riding along. If only Joseph would make a child's saddle like that! After that he would never behave badly to Joseph! He would be good and obedient. Perhaps Joseph would like him then and give the child a saddle.

It was quiet for a long time. Everyone was thinking to himself. Suddenly there was a frightened cry from a little lamb. "A snake!"

Right in the middle of the animals, close to the nose of the smallest lamb, lay a big snake, who lived some way off in a corner of the meadow. How had he managed to get there, without anyone seeing him? They were all terrified!

Then the snake spoke and said: "You have been talking about Mary's child, and yet you are afraid of me. Don't you know, then, that this child can play with snakes without danger? Don't you know, then, that he will care for the wild and the tame animals alike? Don't you know that on Mary's field no living thing can harm any other?"

"Yes," answered the oldest sheep, very ashamed. "You are right. We won't be afraid of you any more. And you too can rejoice with us about Mary's child."

Harvest time

Harvest time came. There really was a great deal for Mary and her little donkey to do.

The figs had to be picked, carried home and laid out to dry on the flat roof. Mary's fig tree was bending under the weight of its fruit, and the baskets which the donkey had to carry were very heavy. But Mary patted him, gave him some sweet figs to chew, and so he didn't feel tired. At last all the figs were gathered.

"Now, my little donkey, we can have a few days' rest before the vintage begins."

"Marvellous," the little donkey thought as he rubbed his head against Mary's arm, "then I can spend the whole day in the meadow with the goats and sheep."

All the same, next morning Mary came into the stable with the yoke. "Little donkey," she said, "our poor neighbour Judith is all alone. She has no donkey. Let's give her a bit of help, you and I."

"It is marvellous in the meadow," the little donkey thought, "but it gives even more pleasure to work the whole day with Mary."

And so he trotted off willingly with her. Judith was delighted to have help.

"I am old and frail," she said. "I didn't think that anyone still bothered about me. But I see that God thinks even about an old woman like me. And he sends me the best woman in all Nazareth."

"And the most intelligent donkey, Judith," laughed Mary.

Then Mary and the donkey worked several days for Judith.

"We have finished now," Mary said one evening.

"Tomorrow I'll be able to spend in the meadow for sure," thought the donkey. "That will be wonderful, wonderful. When I trouble to think about it I know I really am a bit tired."

"The grape picking starts tomorrow," Joseph said when he came home. "It's too bad that you haven't had a good rest, Mary."

"It doesn't matter, Joseph," Mary answered. "After all, I have my hard-working donkey. If you hadn't bought him for me I would have had to drag everything home myself, and then I would have been really tired now. But I was able to help Judith and I am very pleased that I could."

"What a pity," the oldest sheep said to the donkey. "You can't spend a single day enjoying yourself in the meadow."

"It really is wonderful in the meadow," the donkey replied, "but it is even more enjoyable to work with Mary."

"Oh yes, we all understand that," said all the animals.

The vintage was the jolliest time of the whole year. Everywhere poor people in their little gardens and rich people in their great vineyards laughed and sang and picked the juicy grapes.

The animals all felt this happiness. Every day Mary's little donkey tripped along as though it was some sort of dance, although the baskets with the grapes were very heavy.

"What a lot of grapes we're getting this year," said Joseph. "And such beautiful ones too!"

"There's plenty, both for making wine and for drying," Mary replied happily. "But our little donkey is looking tired. He must really have a few days in the meadow to recover and get his strength back before the olive harvest begins."

"Tomorrow we are going to have fun in the meadow, aren't we?" cried the lambs and goats happily.

"Yes, of course," said the donkey.

But early next morning Mary told her donkey: "Judith really has nobody who can help her pick her grapes. They are overripe already. She can't pick them fast enough any more. We two must help her for a few days."

"It's fine to be in the meadow all right," the little donkey thought to himself, "but it's nothing compared to working with Mary."

So he and Mary worked for poor Judith.

"How fortunate it is to have good neighbours," Judith told them. "It is the best present God can give poor people."

Mary replied, "A hard-working donkey is a precious gift too."

And so Judith's grapes were plucked and carried in too, and when that was done it was time for the olive harvest.

"You are not getting any rest," Joseph said.

"That doesn't matter," Mary assured him. "But I'm sorry for the donkey."

"No!" he thought and snuggled up to Mary. "There's nothing better in all the world than going with you."

"I must close my workshop for a few days now and help you," Joseph declared.

The olive harvest was hard work. There was a small wood outside Nazareth where the old, gnarled olive-trees grew and where all the inhabitants had the right to pick olives. The men climbed to the top of the trees and struck down at the olives with long sticks; children collected them when they fell on the ground and filled the baskets with them. The women picked the olives they could reach with their hands. Although the donkey now had to carry terribly heavy baskets he never felt tired.

"You were right, Mary," Joseph said. "That is a really good donkey, the best in the whole town I do believe."

"He's the best in the whole world," insisted Mary.

Out in the olive grove Mary's little donkey met the other donkeys of Nazareth. They didn't recognize him, not even the donkeys of the rich man. Neither did his old drover.

"What a splendid donkey," sighed the rich man's donkeys. "How delicately he trips along! How beautifully he carries his head, so upright and proud! And how clean and well groomed he is!"

"He seems to me to be like a donkey I know," said the oldest donkey. "His gait and bearing were just as handsome. But I can't quite remember who it was."

"He is very handsome, very handsome," marvelled the youngest donkey. "And so strong."

And the old donkey declared: "He ought to be with us, for we belong to a really outstanding man. He isn't really suitable for these poor people."

"I just can't understand where they got him," wondered another of the rich man's donkeys.

Mary's little donkey heard all this and laughed to himself as he made his way home with the baskets. Many times he had to go to and fro between the olive grove and Joseph's house. And several times a day Joseph led the donkey past the house to Judith.

"Joseph, you must do that," Mary had said. "How else can the poor woman get her olives?"

"You are quite right, Mary," Joseph had agreed. "We have been given the best donkey in the whole world and to show our gratitude to God the very least we can do is to help our neighbour. But time flies, and you are not getting any rest."

"It will soon be winter," said Mary. "I can take it easy then, and so can the little donkey."

"What does it matter if I have a rest or if I don't, just so long as I'm allowed to be with Mary," the little donkey thought.

But when the harvest was over the donkey had to accompany Joseph.

The hot weather, which had parched the hills and the valleys, was over. It was getting colder. Joseph took the donkey with him into the countryside to fetch firewood. Until late evening Joseph searched for dry branches, which he tied on to the little donkey. Sometimes his load was higher than he was. They had to go a long way to find anything. There was only a little wood round Nazareth, and the other poor people of the town were out collecting wood too.

One day, when Joseph had gone unusually far with the donkey, black clouds began to gather in the sky. The sun was hidden and it became quite dark, although it was only early afternoon. A cold wind blew in from the sea.

"Now the rainy season is beginning," Joseph thought happily. "The earth need not thirst any longer. Every stream and every spring is filling with water again and the animals can drink as much as they like. This glorious rain!"

Unlike Joseph, the little donkey didn't like the rain. Ugh, no, it was unpleasantly wet and cold. Still, if Joseph said it was good, that must be right. All the same he longed to be home in his warm, dry stable. He pawed the ground impatiently.

"Now, now, little donkey," warned Joseph. "I think

we should perhaps take a little more home today. Quite likely the rain will make us stay at home tomorrow. I know a place a little further north where we can certainly find some wood."

So the donkey had to go still further with Joseph. He was on the point of refusing to move. It occurred to him that it was fun to be disobedient, and to buck and rear. Joseph would find it a hard job to move him, he thought.

Suddenly he remembered the child. The child who later on perhaps would ride on his back. He must be obedient so that Joseph would make a pretty little saddle for him. So he trotted willingly after Joseph.

"You are a dear, hard-working little donkey," Joseph praised him. "Perhaps you do understand that we have to gather a lot of firewood for Mary's sake. She must keep the house warm so that our little child doesn't freeze." At this the donkey felt ashamed of his ugly thoughts.

When they reached the place Joseph had spoken about they found plenty of twigs. Joseph loaded up as much as the donkey could carry.

"Now we'll go back," said Joseph. "I'll walk beside you and hold the load steady."

Meanwhile evening had come on. The wind blew right through them, and it started to rain. It was a real cloudburst. The rain beat into their eyes so that both of them could scarcely see anything. They advanced with difficulty. And then Joseph lost his way. He stood still and tried to pick out the path. It was impossible. Joseph and the donkey were lost.

"We must keep more to the left," Joseph thought and pulled the reins. But the little donkey wanted to go to the right. That was the way they had come. Why did Joseph want to go in the opposite direction?

"Come on!" cried Joseph and he pulled with all his strength.

Thereupon the little donkey squatted on his hind legs. Not a single step in the wrong direction!

"Don't turn stubborn now of all times," begged Joseph. "You have been so good and understanding. We must stick together if we are to get home to Mary before it is night."

That was just what the donkey wanted to do. However much Joseph pulled, he remained rooted to the spot. Joseph let go of the reins for a moment in order to fasten some branches of wood which had become loose. The donkey was waiting for this. Quick as lightning he straightened up and trotted off to the right.

Joseph leaped after him and shouted, "Halt! Stop! We'll get lost. Stop!"

The donkey let Joseph come nearly close enough to get hold of him and then trotted quickly away from him again. Joseph had to go on following, although he was worn out and troubled. He was afraid he might lose Mary's little donkey.

Suddenly the donkey stopped and uttered a cry. In the darkness Joseph could scarcely recognize him any more but he heard his triumphant "Hee-haw!"

Joseph then succeeded in getting hold of his reins. He looked round and was utterly astounded. They were standing right in front of the town gate of Nazareth! "Well, I never!" Joseph thought. "Can I really believe my own eyes? We are in Nazareth! Mary was right. You are the most intelligent donkey in the whole world."

Mary was at home, sitting in the warm stable and milking. The lambs and the goats gave her no peace. They nudged and jostled her, they pawed her knees with their hooves, all just to make her pat them and stroke them. The older animals tried to keep their young ones under control and rebuked them for troubling her.

"Don't stop them," Mary said. "They are so sweet and they'll grow quiet enough when they are older. And that happens very quickly. But what has kept Joseph and the donkey this evening? They must have been caught in the rain. I would be worried if I didn't know that the angels are protecting them."

At that very moment the stable door opened. Joseph and the donkey came in. Mary stood up and helped Joseph to unload the heavy load of wood and she dried the wet donkey. Joseph took off his soaking cloak and explained how he had lost the way and the donkey had found the right way and forced him to follow behind.

Mary laughed and said she had always known that her donkey was the cleverest donkey in the whole world.

And all the animals in the stable looked in wonder at the donkey and the oldest sheep said, "My children, there is a lesson for you all in this!"

"Yes," the lambs and goats bleated, "our donkey is very, very clever and a great hero."

"Oh, nonsense," the little donkey said. "I only wanted to get back to Mary as quickly as possible. That's why I took the right road home."

That night, just as on every other night, the animals in the stable talked about Mary's little child. Thereupon the donkey quite forgot how very cold and tired he was.

"Isn't it coming soon, mother?" cried the lambs anxiously.

"Do you think it will come tomorrow?" bleated the impatient little goats.

"It will be a little while yet," answered the older animals.

"But only just a tiny, little bit longer", said a little lamb excitedly. "A weeny, teeny little bit."

"Be good, children, and go to sleep now," commanded the oldest sheep. "Otherwise it will be a terribly long time."

None of them dared then to go on talking. The lambs and little goats dreamed about the child. But the donkey dreamt about Mary.

The Emperor's decree

The next day it rained cats and dogs. The donkey was able to stay with his friends in the stable and rest. He thought it was marvellous to be able to rest at last.

In the evening Joseph came in when Mary was milking.

"Terrible weather!" he said. "It's a good thing we have managed to get everything in, all the harvest and the wood for the winter."

"Yes, we are lucky," Mary replied. "Joseph, do you think we could spare Judith a little wood?"

Joseph thought about this. "I think I could let her have one donkey load tomorrow," he said.

"That will please her," laughed Mary.

"You are right, Mary. I will . . ."

Just then there was a loud knock on the door. Joseph went and opened it. He stayed outside for some time, and when he came back, he looked worried and troubled.

"Who was it?" Mary asked anxiously. "Was it something bad?"

"We must travel to Bethlehem immediately!" Joseph said.

"Bethlehem? That is a long way. What have we to do in Bethlehem?"

"The Emperor has decreed that all the people in his Empire are to be counted," explained Joseph. "Everyone is to be written in big books and every man must go to the town from which his family comes."

"But couldn't we be written just as well in the book here in Nazareth?"

"No, it has to be done in the town of each man's ancestors, for that is what the Emperor has ordered. I belong to the house of David in Bethlehem, and that is why we must go there."

"But I can't go just now," Mary said. "My child may really be born any day now."

The lambs suddenly became very excited, but neither Mary nor Joseph noticed.

"Sh!" warned the oldest sheep.

"The Emperor has ordered everyone to travel at once," Joseph said. "We cannot put off the journey."

"Joseph dear, then you must go alone. You surely don't want the child to be born by the roadside? Or even among wild beasts in the wilderness?"

"Perhaps we can get to Bethlehem in time," Joseph said to comfort her.

"But," complained Mary, "we don't know anyone there with whom we can stay."

"I feel very worried, Mary," Joseph said gently. "But you must come with me. The Emperor has ordered that everybody must go. His scribe wants to see every member of each family before he makes an entry. And the Emperor must be obeyed."

Mary sat down and thought about the problem. Suddenly she stood up and said, "It may be all right after all. We have our fine donkey, haven't we? Who knows, perhaps God gave him to us just for this journey. I'll pack up all the child's things, and a warm fur for him to sleep in, and plenty of food for the journey. The donkey must carry all that and me too when I get tired."

"But who is going to look after all our animals while we are away?" pondered Joseph.

"I will go and see my sister tomorrow and ask her. Her husband is a Nazareth man, so they won't have to leave. She'll certainly look after the animals for us gladly, as long as we are away. I believe everything is going to be all right, Joseph."

Mary went into the house and prepared the supper. Joseph shut the stable carefully so that no wild animals could get in and steal the cattle. Then he too left the stable.

But the whole stable was in a state of shock. The animals had heard everything but without understanding it all. The lambs and little goats had only noticed what Mary had said about the child being born soon. The bigger animals had understood, though, that something was not quite right.

"It's going to come now, to come now," cried the small animals.

"But not here," replied the oldest sheep. "Joseph clearly said that they must go on a long journey, and that Mary had to go too."

"Well, the child can stay all right with us here," the little goats cried.

"I've never heard anything quite so stupid," grumbled the old sheep. "Mothers don't leave their children behind and go off on a journey. Anyway, the child hasn't been born yet."

"Does Mary have to leave then, just when the child is at last going to be born?" wailed the lambs and the little goats, who understood at last, although they still didn't want to believe it. "That isn't right."

"Be patient," the older animals advised. "Haven't you heard Mary say she would come back."

"But that will take a long time," wailed the young ones.

"And what if they never find the way home again?" the youngest lamb asked.

"Our clever donkey is to go with them," the oldest sheep answered. "So there is no danger of that."

"No, no danger," the little ones agreed. "But hurry as much as you can, little donkey."

"I'll do that," the donkey assured them. "I'll go as carefully as possible too so that the child is not hurt at all. We'll soon be back, and then everything will be fine. Now go to sleep."

Gradually the lambs and little goats calmed down, and so did the big animals. Soon everyone, human and animal, in Mary's house was asleep.

For some days Mary and Joseph worked untiringly. The little donkey was allowed to stay in the stable most of the time.

"Have a thorough rest," Mary said. "It's a long, long way to Bethlehem."

Joseph completed all the orders he had for people in Nazareth. Then he delivered them to his customers. When that was done, he swept out the workshop, cleaned his tools and locked up.

Meanwhile Mary baked bread and packed it up along with pressed, dry figs, olive oil and other good things in a hamper.

Then she put together all the things she had sewn for the child, the shawl and swaddling clothes and the little shirts. How delicately beautiful they were! She spread them all out on the table and looked at them. She called Joseph then, for he too had to admire them. Then she bundled them all up in a white sheepskin.

When she was ready to leave, Mary brushed and mended her own and Joseph's clothes so that they both should be neat and clean when they travelled to strange places.

She visited her sister, of course, and asked her to look after the animals. Her sister was very sad that Mary had to leave Nazareth and she gladly undertook to take care of the beasts. Even old Judith offered to help.

"I had always hoped I would be allowed to rock your son in his cradle, but now instead of that I'll look after your lambs."

"Thank you, Judith," Mary replied. "That pleases me very much."

On the last evening before she left, the animals pressed more strongly against Mary than usual when she sat down and was going to milk.

"My dears," Mary said, "do you know then that I must go away? I see it in your eyes. Don't be sad. My sister has promised to be good to you. And so has old Judith. Besides, Judith has plenty of time: she can tell you plenty of stories and spoil you, for she has nothing else to do. My sister is always in too much of a hurry to do that."

Then all the animals bleated, but they sounded dreadfully miserable and sad.

"Now, listen," said Mary. "I'll come back soon. And then, oh then, I'll be carrying my little son in my arms. Listen, you rogues, you'll have to be careful then, and not push and shove, for he'll be small and delicate, and unable to stand hard knocks. Now be really good all the time I'm away. But you must learn to wait patiently, for it will certainly be some time."

Mary said good-bye to them that evening. "You won't be awake tomorrow morning when we leave," she said.

But they were all awake, all of them, and watching Joseph miserably while he loaded the donkey and fastened all the baggage safely on him.

"Don't be sad," the little donkey said comfortingly to his friends, "we are going away now, but we shall soon come back."

"Take good care of Mary and her child," urged the animals.

"I promise to do that," the donkey answered solemnly.

"Come on now," Joseph said and he lifted Mary into the saddle. "We must be off. It is still dark, but it will soon be light. Wrap your shawl well round you, Mary, for the wind is cold this morning."

And so Joseph, Mary and the little donkey set out on the long journey to Bethlehem.

On the road to Bethlehem

It was a long way from Nazareth to Bethlehem. It took the little donkey nearly a whole week, although he trotted along gamely from early to late.

The donkey was proud, though, of being able to carry Mary on his back all day, and with head held high he tripped along as gracefully and spiritedly as ever.

"Joseph, I am so pleased with our donkey," Mary said. "I could not have gone all the way without him. What a good thing it was that you bought him for me."

For the first few days the road went through places they knew. They went past the fields and pastures, the vineyards, olive orchards and fig-tree plantations of Nazareth. Then they came to strange villages but these were very similar to Nazareth.

Sometimes it poured with rain. Mary and Joseph were glad when it rained, because plenty of rain is good for both plants and animals. Sometimes the sun shone, and they were glad that they could dry their wet clothes and warm their cold, frozen limbs.

In time they came to a stream which had burst its banks after heavy rain. Usually it was just a narrow little stream which could easily be crossed. But today it was a wide, roaring torrent!

Joseph was worried and stood and stroked his beard thoughtfully.

How could they get across?

He girt his long cloak round his hips. Then he

cautiously advanced one step into the water. Woosh! The stream could easily have dragged him along. Joseph quickly pulled himself back on to the bank.

"If I only knew what we ought to do," Joseph was thinking. "I hardly think the donkey can cross there! We must wait until the water subsides. But that can take days."

"I believe that God will show us a way," Mary said confidently.

"Joseph, look at our donkey!"

The little donkey suddenly began to prance along the bank, with Mary still on his back. He had seen a shining figure which beckoned him, and he was following it. It was an angel, but neither Joseph nor Mary could see it.

When the donkey reached the angel, the angel grasped the reins and led the donkey into the water.

"Stop! Stop! Donkey!" shouted the terrified Joseph. "Pull him back, Mary!"

But the donkey was wading through the water. The angel guided him to the opposite bank over some large, flat stones. Joseph could see no stones, of course, for the water was pouring over them, but he rushed after the donkey and reached the opposite bank just as safely.

"Mary," he cried, "were you very frightened?"

"Frightened?" Mary asked in surprise. "What should I be afraid of? I believe the angel of God was guiding the donkey, although I could not see him."

"You may well be right, Mary," said Joseph. "It really was stupid of me to be so afraid. How my heart pounded!"

Soon it was midday. Mary dismounted from the donkey. They ate and rested themselves under a fig tree which had many new buds. Joseph found some

winter figs which were fit to eat and gave them to
Mary.

"You see," Mary said. "This rain really suits these
trees. They don't look so dry and withered any more.
There is new life in them."

Just at that moment the air became full of the joyous
song of many birds. A flock of birds had settled in the
tree and were singing with all their heart.

"How happy they are," Mary said. "Can you hear
them singing about my child?"

Joseph laughed. "How do you know that?"

"I just know," Mary said mysteriously. "But Joseph,
haven't you noticed? They are our birds."

43

"Our birds?"

"Yes, don't you recognize them? They are the birds from our garden in Nazareth. I know them again. That one is the little one who always jumps sideways, and there's the tame one, look, who isn't afraid to eat out of my hand. Don't you recognize them, Joseph? And I know that one too! And that one, and that one! Yes, they are all there. Oh, Joseph, they have flown after us. They want to be there to greet the child."

"Are you quite certain that they are our birds?" asked Joseph, who felt that he recognized them too.

"Quite sure," Mary said. "That's right, isn't it, my little donkey. You recognize them too, don't you?"

Yes, the little donkey recognized them. He had noticed, too, for a long time that they were following. Sometimes they had flown on ahead, sometimes they kept behind, and sometimes they were sitting on a tree and chirping as the donkey trotted by, and occasionally they flew along close to Mary. The donkey only wondered why Mary had not recognized them earlier.

After the rest they all travelled on until it was evening. It was hard keeping going for so many hours. All three were tired out when the sun set.

"We should not go any further now," Joseph declared. "We must look for somewhere where we can spend the night."

"In a house if possible, Joseph," Mary pleaded.

"Are you cold? Perhaps we can manage to keep going a bit longer and reach a village soon," Joseph said.

It was getting dark quickly as they struggled on, and Joseph was afraid that they wouldn't find a house and would be forced after all to spend the night in the open.

44

"Don't worry, Joseph," Mary said. "I believe that God will help us."

Scarcely had she spoken these words when an angel again appeared to the donkey and beckoned him eagerly. The donkey ran towards him and on to a small hillock. From there a faint light could be seen quite near them.

"Joseph, a village! God be praised!" cried Mary happily.

The travellers soon reached the village. Joseph knocked at the door of the first house and asked for shelter. The people of the house were quite poor. The husband invited them to come in, and the housewife asked them to share supper with them.

Soon Mary, Joseph and the donkey were fast asleep in the strange house.

In the morning they were all wakened by the singing of the birds.

"What birds are those?" the man asked.

"They are my birds," Mary told him. "They flew along with us because they want to welcome my child with their happy cries the moment he comes into the world."

"Birds from Nazareth?" asked the man in astonishment.

"What kind of a child is going to be born then," asked the woman, "if the birds fly such a long way just to sing at his birth? Is there something special about this child?"

Mary smiled and nodded mysteriously.

"You must come to us again and show us the child on your way back," urged the woman.

"Gladly," Mary said.

Meanwhile the children of these poor people had made friends with the little donkey. They had helped Joseph to groom him, had given him hay and water and didn't want to be parted from him. One small boy started to cry. "Mother, can't we buy a donkey like this," he sobbed.

"We can't do that," said the mother. "But when you are big enough you can earn yourself enough money to buy one."

"But we want to have him now and ride him sometimes," wailed the boy.

The other children did not speak. They stood all round the little donkey very shyly and stroked him wherever they could touch him.

"Let the little ones come a little way with us," Joseph suggested, "and then they can have a short ride."

46

Their mother laughed and agreed.

What joy there was!

Joseph lifted the smallest child up to Mary and the whole throng moved forward singing and shouting with joy. Joseph let the oldest boy lead the donkey and he came last himself.

After a while Mary gave the smallest child to its sister and lifted up the boy who had cried so bitterly before. Now he boldly clicked with his tongue to make the donkey go faster and was indeed so excited and playful that Mary had some trouble in holding him.

In this way all the children had their turn riding the donkey. They had gone a really long way from their home before they had finished. The company rested then and Mary let the little ones share her morning snack.

"Now we must send you all home so that your parents don't start to worry," Mary declared.

"We have never had so much fun," said the oldest sister. "Mary is a dear."

"So is the donkey," cried the cheeky small boy.

"And Joseph," they all agreed.

"Will you really come back?" they asked. "May we travel along with you again?"

Joseph promised that they would.

"May I still lead the donkey then?" the small boy asked. "By that time I shall have grown a whole lot bigger."

"Yes," Joseph said, "you shall lead him a fair way."

"I'll collect some juicy grass for him every day," the little boy declared, "a really big heap. That's how good a time you'll have with me, little donkey."

"With us too," the others assured him.

The oldest sister shyly asked, "When you return, will you let me just carry the little child?"

"Most certainly. I have noticed how you treat your smaller brothers and sisters. See that they all get home safely. Otherwise I shall worry about you all. You have a long way to go to reach home now."

At last the children said good-bye and went. But for as long as Joseph, Mary and the donkey could see them they were walking backwards and waving. Towards evening the travellers came to a very lonely district. The villages were a long way from each other.

"I am afraid that we shall have to spend tonight in the open," Joseph said sadly. "From here we have a good view in all directions but I can't see any lights whichever way I look. Do you think you will get terribly cold, Mary?"

"As long as it doesn't start to rain," Mary replied, "it will be all right. But, it is a clear, starry night. Although the wind is cold, we can wrap ourselves up in the shawl."

Joseph helped Mary down from the donkey. She sat down by the side of the road and Joseph saw that she was shivering with cold. He took off his cloak and put it round her.

"Don't," said Mary. "You are freezing just as much as I."

"You keep it to begin with," Joseph pleaded. "I'll look around for somewhere sheltered from the wind."

"Yes, God will certainly let us sleep well this night too," Mary said. "But just where is the donkey?"

"Hee-haw!" come the answer out of the darkness.

Once more the donkey had caught sight of an angel, who had shown him a grotto quite near. It was obvious that travellers frequently spent the night there as there was some straw on the ground and one or two dry logs by a burnt-out fireplace. How delighted Joseph was when he saw in the pale light of the stars what the donkey had discovered. He fetched Mary and piled up straw to make her a couch. He made fire, and lit one or two logs. It was really warm and comfortable in the dark grotto.

"How God does protect us, Joseph," said Mary. "Every night we find a couch, even in the middle of the wilderness."

They slept peacefully and in safety until the birds woke them at sunrise.

In the robbers' den

Day after day Joseph, Mary and their little donkey travelled on along the road to Bethlehem. Sometimes things looked bad for them, but each time the angel showed the little donkey what to do.

But once the donkey gave them a fright.

The travellers were making their way across a lonely district. Early in the afternoon they came to a village. They drew water from the well and while they were resting Joseph said, "Do we want to go any further today? I am afraid that it is a very long way to the next place. We may not reach it before dark."

"But don't you think that it is still too early to look for a place to spend the night," Mary answered. "The nearer we are to Bethlehem the better it is for us."

"I'll ask this woman I see coming," Joseph said.

"If you keep up a good speed you could reach the next village before nightfall," the woman said and looked at them with curiosity. "But the road is difficult, steep and very stony. Ah well, but your donkey looks strong, he should be able to make it."

"He is the best donkey in the world," said Mary.

"But there are robbers along the road," the woman added. "They live in the wild mountains. They are very dangerous if you fall into their hands. Perhaps you had better wait until tomorrow. Some peasants from this village are going to Jerusalem, and you could join them. The robbers don't dare to attack if there are a lot of people."

"Yes," agreed Joseph, "it probably is best for us to

wait. Is it quite certain that these peasants will be travelling tomorrow?"

"I think so," answered the woman. "Or the day after tomorrow."

"Shouldn't we try then to reach the next place," Mary said. "It is still quite early in the afternoon. Our little donkey is reliable. And God will protect us from the robbers."

So they travelled on. It had been such a beautiful day when they set out but an hour or so later the wind suddenly got up and a terrible cloud-burst took them by surprise. In a trice the darkness was complete, and this was just at the most difficult part of the road.

The donkey had to go ahead with Mary and had to grope with his hoofs for the safest path. Joseph climbed behind them, for the road was very narrow.

"We must find some shelter," cried Joseph. "This wind is blowing right through you."

But the donkey didn't find any shelter and Mary began to freeze with cold.

"We must stop soon, even if we don't come to any houses," Joseph was thinking.

Before his very eyes the donkey suddenly disappeared. He had to run to catch up with him.

Once more the donkey had seen an angel. The angel beckoned him to the far side of a gigantic boulder. A narrower path ran along there and a little way along it the donkey came to a hut.

"Joseph! There's a hut here!" Mary called, and tried to turn round in his direction. Joseph was panting along behind them.

The donkey was already close to the hut. It was only a rickety shack without a door. But a fire was burning on the floor and three men sat round it, warming themselves. When they caught sight of the donkey one of them jumped up, seized the reins and led the donkey into the hut.

How delighted the donkey was that in this terrible weather Mary at last had a roof over her head.

"Good people, permit us to warm ourselves a little," Mary asked them, "we are wet through and through."

The men at first did not answer.

Mary did not look at them at all carefully, for her eyes were on the fire and she stretched her hands out towards it. But Joseph, who came in at this moment, saw what kind of people these three men were. Their little donkey had led them right into the robbers' den!

"Good people," Mary implored them, "we don't want to give you any trouble, but please let us just sit by your fire."

"Come on then," one of them said roughly.

Mary stretched her hands out towards him and so he had to help her down from the donkey's back. And at that moment he had the feeling that the fire burnt more brightly and the air in the shack had the fragrance of a spring day. Mary sank down on the straw on the floor. Joseph still hesitated at the door. He didn't know what to do for the best.

"Joseph, pass me down the box with the food," Mary asked him. "You must be hungry too."

Joseph fetched the food and Mary took out the loaf. She broke it in pieces and said, "Lord, bless our bread!"

She passed a slice of bread to Joseph and passed some to the three robbers. These three were so embarrassed that they could scarcely eat. It was a very long time since they had eaten bread that had been blessed!

Mary and Joseph ate and the little donkey started to nibble at the straw on the floor.

The three robbers continued to sit still and watch the strangers. They could not understand how anyone could find their hidden shack. All the same it was useful to have people coming straight to them. All they had to do was to take their luggage while they were sleeping and then sneak out with the donkey. There was no need to use force at all.

The three robbers looked and winked at each other. Joseph realized what sort of people they were. He looked worried and could hardly swallow his food. But Mary seemed quite unaware. She looked at the robbers with wonderfully bright eyes and smiled at them as if they were good, old friends.

When she had finished eating Mary dried the donkey and said, "You just don't know what a clever donkey this is!"

And she started to tell them how the donkey had waded across the river that had burst its banks and how he found a resting place for them every night.

"But this evening we had started to think that we must spend the night in the open. It was surely an angel who showed our little donkey the path. Without an angel we should never have found this hut right out in these lonely mountains," she told them.

The robbers listened to her in astonishment. They thought that this was a very childish woman. What angel would have led their donkey into a robbers' hide-out, of all places. She must be easy to fool.

Then an idea came to the robber chief which struck him with terror. He became quite pale and broke out into a cold sweat.

There was something unusual about this woman and he had noticed this from the beginning. When he helped her down from the donkey everything near her had been bright and lovely. It wasn't the fire that had burnt brighter, although that was what he had believed at first! No, he knew what it was now. Another being had been with her, and from this other being the light and warmth had poured. An angel. And after that, he had sat there making wicked plans against people who were watched over by an angel! He went cold at the thought of what would have happened to him and his comrades if they had lifted a hand against these people. Luckily the woman had spoken before they had been able to do her any harm. He must see to it that his comrades left these strangers in peace.

The two other robbers laughed mockingly as they listened to the lively, innocent story of the woman.

Then a bird chirped quite unexpectedly. Mary interrupted her story and cried out, "Listen, Joseph! Our birds have found the way here!"

And then she began to tell the even more miraculous story of the birds of Nazareth. She told them how the birds had flown after her for the whole journey so that they could greet her child as soon as he was born into the world. Whenever they rested the birds sat in a tree and sang for her, and every morning they woke her with a song.

The men thought the woman was unbelievably childish, but they could not help listening to her. But when they looked up they saw that the beams and rafters were full of sleeping birds.

The second robber was a rough fellow. He had no respect for anything and struck out without pity to get whatever he wanted. But as a small boy he had been crazy about birds and he had always been very good at handling them.

He stared at Mary's birds like a man bewitched. Hardly aware of what he was doing, he collected some breadcrumbs and held them out in his outstretched hand. Then he whistled softly. One or two heads came out from hiding under their wings. Two or three birds flew out and circled round him, but they were uneasy. They looked at Mary as though asking her advice. Should they? Mary nodded. The boldest one, the little one who hopped sideways, flew on to the robber's

54

hand and pecked at a tiny crumb. In a flash he had the whole flock round him. They settled on his hands, on his shoulders and on his head, twittering and chirping.

The robber sat quite still, so as not to scare them away.

"How I have longed for birds," he said. "For bird-song. Here in the mountains you only hear the vulture's shriek."

"Do you like these birds?" Mary asked.

The robber became friendly then and asked Mary and Joseph the names of the birds and where they made their nests and how many little ones they had usually and a whole lot more. He wanted to know more than they could tell him.

"I can't understand," he thought, "why I have stayed so long in these barren mountains. Tomorrow I'm going to go to some place where there are trees and birds. I'll stay there and earn my living with the work of my hands. But for these strangers with their birds I would have stayed here till my dying day. I am so glad you came. I will see to it that my comrades leave you in peace. How happy birds have always made me!"

The youngest robber hadn't asked about angels or birds. He was quite young, and had only come across the other two not long ago. He came from a good home but had always been wild and unruly. He always wanted to come first and to be the best. And one day someone else acquired greater honour than he in his village. In his rage he left the village and joined the robbers to make himself a name as "Terror of the Wilds". He was going to show the people of his village! They were to go in fear of him and tremble at his name! He had always been very wild and fierce when he and his companions were looting and robbing.

Now he sat and grew angry with his comrades. He

saw clearly that they were both being charmed by the strange woman and thinking of having pity on her and her husband.

"You poor old fools!" he thought angrily. "Soon you too will be like children again and too feeble to go robbing any more. All right, that doesn't matter. Tonight when everyone is sleeping I'll take the luggage and the donkey and disappear."

Then he began to imagine what could be in the luggage. Something valuable, for sure.

He could feel that in some way or other the strangers were unusual. Quite likely they were not so poor as they seemed. The woman had a well-bred look. Now he knew what it was. She was in disguise. She probably thought that she could carry her jewels through the countryside more safely if she looked like a beggar woman and hid everything in a rough bundle. But he saw through it all! They couldn't fool him! And this donkey certainly did not belong to poor people! No!

There were some very valuable things in that bundle, he was sure. And tomorrow it would all belong to him! A long way away he was going to open it and be a rich man. And then he was going to collect a gang of wild dare-devils round him and be a robber chieftain. The "Terror of the Wilds"! They'd hear from him at home in his own village! If only these people would lie down and go to sleep. Sitting up and chattering the whole night!

He was so full of impatience that he was biting his nails all the time. Ah, well, it would soon be quiet.

But once more the oldest robber could not stay silent. "Who are you really?" he asked Mary. "Birds fly after you, but an angel leads your donkey straight into a robbers' den."

"I am only Mary of Nazareth," Mary explained, "and Joseph is simply Joseph. It's not for our sakes that the birds fly after us and the angels protect us. It's for the sake of the child who is going to be born soon."

"A little child?" whispered the old robber.

Mary nodded and smiled at him. And at that moment the fear with which the appearance of the angel had filled him left him. He felt well and happy.

"Wonderful," he thought.

"Here, I'll show you something really beautiful," Mary said mysteriously to the robber. "Joseph, please help me to get the luggage down."

Joseph undid the straps. The youngest robber held his breath in his excitement. His right hand clutched the handle of his dagger so fiercely that his knuckles were quite white.

What kind of jewels did this woman have? What was she so proud of?

She sat down and put the bundle on her lap. When she had brushed all the pieces of straw from her dress she took out one or two small child's things and showed them to the astonished robbers.

"Look!" she said and passed each of them a tiny little shirt. "Are they not perfect?"

The youngest robber was so taken aback that he let his dagger fall to the ground.

Joseph saw it and quick as lightning pushed it with his foot into the straw. But the robber didn't notice this at all. He stood there, twisting and turning the little shirt this way and that and getting redder and redder in the face.

What a disgrace! Supposing he had stolen this bundle with the little child's clothes! What laughter there would have been from town to town, from village to village. The smallest child would have laughed at the mere mention of his name. The "Terror of the Wilds", who stole the laundry of a new born baby! Oh!

He threw the little shirt into Mary's lap. Mary carefully folded the child's clothes up again. Everyone was silent.

Then the young man started to speak. "I wanted to be a hero. But you don't become famous for stealing the clothes of a child who has not yet been born. Tell your child when he grows up that the 'Terror of the Wilds' was planning to steal his baby clothes. Then he'll know how evil men are."

"My son is coming to help those who have taken a wrong path," Mary said.

"Tell him this," the young man cried. "Yes, yes, I'll make a fresh start and become an honest man. You can't win fame and honour as a robber. 'Terror of the Wilds' Ha! Ha! How stupid I have been."

"I'll come with you," said the old robber.

"I don't want to stay here any longer either," said the man with the birds. "I had already made up my mind to go somewhere tomorrow where there are trees and the song of birds."

"Mary of Nazareth," said the old robber, "tell your child that because of him the three wickedest robbers left these barren mountains and set out to become decent human beings."

"I shall tell him," Mary replied smiling, "that three good men took pity in a terrible storm on two travellers and their little donkey."

Then they all slept quietly through the night in the robbers' den. And next morning the birds of Nazareth sang for three happy men who were not robbers any more.

"I'll show you the best way to the next village," the young man said.

He took the donkey's reins and led him along an almost hidden path until a village could be seen in the distance.

"Thank you, Mary's dear little donkey, for coming to us last night," he said.

He stroked the donkey and gave him a farewell pat and said good-bye to Mary and Joseph. They wished him good luck. After that he returned to his comrades who were already packing their few belongings for the journey to another country.

With the shepherds

"Mary," Joseph said that day, "do you know, I think we shall reach Bethlehem tomorrow, if all goes well."

"That would be marvellous," sighed Mary. "The little child is not going to wait any longer. How good it will be to have a roof over our heads again."

"Aha," thought the little donkey, "if that's how things are, I must hurry." And he started to trot, trot along so that Joseph had to keep running beside him to keep up with him.

"It's remarkable that our donkey is so strong still," Mary said thoughtfully. "He had to work so hard all through the harvest and yet he has carried me for days from dawn to dusk on his back."

"Yes . . . yes," Joseph panted. "I don't know . . . how . . . he . . . keeps . . . it . . . up."

They travelled on past fields. Again and again they came across large flocks of sheep and herds of goats. They saw no houses, only little huts for the shepherds and low, stone pens in which the beasts spent the nights.

Joseph stood before one of these stone walls that evening. Many, many animals had been herded together and were lying close to each other side by side. The shepherds had made a fire and were sitting by it and warming themselves. One of them kept watch. He had wrapped himself in a sheepskin and was lying right across the middle of the entrance. Anyone who wanted to go in had to step over him. But anyone who tried to do this would be chased away. This would happen to whoever came at night, be it a wild beast who wanted to carry off sheep, or a thief who wanted to steal goats.

Joseph approached the entrance. The shepherd stirred warily.

"What do you want?" he asked gruffly.

"May we spend the night with you? We can't manage to reach Bethlehem."

"Yes," said the shepherd after looking keenly at Joseph from head to foot, "come in. We have no tent, only a fire. If you like to be content with that . . ."

He stood up and led Joseph, the donkey and Mary in.

A twelve-year-old boy came running towards them. "Let me look after the donkey," he asked eagerly. "What a lovely animal. But he's very wet. Has he been sweating?"

"Yes, he has been in such a hurry all day," explained Joseph and he dried his own forehead. "It's good that we can rest now."

The boy rubbed the donkey down with dry grass, gave him hay and fresh water, stroked him, spoke quietly to him and looked after him in every way as well as he could. When he saw that he was freezing in the cold night air he took his own cloak off and spread it over the donkey's back.

"Reuben, what are you doing?" called his grandfather.

"The little donkey is very cold. He was quite wet with sweat," the boy replied. "I don't need a cloak. I'm never cold."

His grandfather shook his head and told him to come to the fire and sit down.

Reuben obeyed him and the old man wrapped his own cloak round the boy.

When the shepherds noticed how tired and cold Mary was they said, "You can't spend the night lying on the open ground. It is going to be cold tonight, the stars are shining unusually brightly.''

One of the shepherds had already fetched one or two goatskins and they all helped to make a small, warm tent with them, a tent just big enough for Mary. Inside the tent they spread a sheepskin on the ground, and another shepherd brought some goat's milk. Mary accepted all these things very gratefully. Then she lay down on the soft sheepskin and fell asleep immediately. She was too tired that evening to sit up and talk as she had done the previous evening in the robbers' den.

But Joseph squatted with the shepherds by the fire for a long time. He told them all about their journey and their adventures. The shepherds listened very attentively, and when he told them how an angel had always shown the donkey the right way, they nodded solemnly.

"Did you see the angel?'' they asked.

"No, neither I nor Mary. But she was aware of it, whenever an angel was close.''

"Yes,'' the old man said thoughtfully. "Good people can feel the presence of an angel, although they can't see him.''

"Our forefathers often talked to angels,'' another man remembered.

"The angels have helped us until now,'' said Joseph, "and we hope they will guide us to Bethlehem too, before Mary's child comes into the world.''

"In Bethlehem,'' explained the old grandfather proudly (for he and all the shepherds came from there) "in Bethlehem King David was born. He guarded his father's flocks as a boy, and when he grew up he became the King and Shepherd of the whole nation.''

"We are all of his line,'' Reuben's father added.

"We are too,'' said Joseph. "And that is why we

have to go to Bethlehem. We are to be counted there."

"Yes, indeed," said another shepherd and he added, "David was born in Bethlehem, but we are still waiting for another King; he was promised to our forefathers by God."

"Reuben, tell us what the prophet says about the child of Bethlehem," urged his grandfather.

"From you, O Bethlehem, shall come forth for me one who is to be ruler over my people," rang out Reuben's clear voice.

"It is also written," said Joseph softly," that he will be the Good Shepherd."

"Who shall lead all peoples along God's path," added Reuben eagerly.

"Yes," one of the shepherds said. "So it is written. But he never comes, although we need him. The years come and go and everything stays the same."

The old grandfather spoke again. "It has always been my strong desire to live to see the child of Bethlehem. It is now unfortunately too late for him to come in my lifetime."

All the shepherds sighed. They had eagerly awaited the Good Shepherd for a long time.

Reuben said shyly, "Do you know, Grandfather, I believe he is coming soon. I can feel that this is so."

"Little boy," the old man replied, "how can you know that?"

"Because something very strange happened just now," said Reuben. "When I was spreading my cloak over the donkey's back his eyes had a strange gleam. I have never seen anything like it, and I was astonished. But then I noticed that the stars were mirrored in his eyes. I turned round and looked up into the sky and the stars were shining so brightly you could almost hear them. It really was like that. And I believe they were singing, "Soon! Soon! Soon!" Then I looked at the donkey again. He knew too that something will happen soon. The Good Shepherd is coming now, that's certain."

"Reuben, you must take care, and not let your imagination get the better of you," the boy's father said sternly.

"Who knows, Reuben may be right," his grandfather suggested. "The stars are certainly unusually bright tonight."

After that there was quiet round the fire. One after another the shepherds wrapped themselves in their cloaks and fell asleep.

Only the little donkey was unable to sleep. Oh dear,

he was so excited by Mary's words, that the child would soon be coming. She really had not the time to spend the whole night resting here and letting hour after hour slip by.

"Little donkey, why are you standing there stamping your hoof?" a sheep asked. "Why don't you sleep?"

"I can't," sighed the donkey. "I can't help thinking all the time about Mary's child. We have waited for it a long time already, you know, and today she said that it would not make her wait any longer. Besides, I promised the other animals at home that I would carry Mary safely and in good time into Bethlehem. Suppose we don't get there . . . Just think of it, the child being born by the roadside. If only I could wake Joseph and Mary up and hurry on with them."

"The night is too dark," remarked another sheep, who had been listening.

"The angels would show me the way."

"Have you seen an angel tonight?" argued the first sheep. "Has one beckoned you? If one had, you would have had to follow immediately."

"No," admitted the donkey. "No, I just haven't seen one."

"Then the angels certainly think that you should rest here for the night," the sheep said.

"Yes, and look how warm and comfortable the shepherds have made everything for the woman."

"Yes, and see how well she is sleeping," added another sheep. "And her husband is sleeping too. He too needs sleep, he was terribly tired when he arrived here."

"Yes," sighed the donkey, "you are right. I only hope they wake up in good time."

They were all up early the next morning. The shepherds invited Joseph and Mary to their early morning meal, and the little donkey was given an armful of hay by Reuben. The birds of Nazareth sang their happiest morning song.

"Now you haven't far to go to reach Bethlehem," Reuben's grandfather said. "You'll be there by midday. You'll find it hard though to find somewhere to stay, for an immense number of people of David's line have come by the Emperor's order. All the same, I expect you'll be all right. And when you come back along this road, we hope you'll pay us a visit, for we are eager to see the child who is to be born in Bethlehem. A child of the line of David!"

Mary gladly promised to do this.

"And I'll have hay and fresh water ready again then for your donkey," Reuben promised. "He is the finest donkey I know."

"You are a good boy, Reuben," Joseph said. "May God be with you always."

Then Joseph and Mary said good-bye to the shepherds and travelled on.

But on this day they had a lot of bad luck.

First of all, there was cold rain and they were soaked right through. After the rain the sky remained cloudy and grey for the rest of the day. No sun broke through to dry their clothes and warm their frozen limbs.

Then the little donkey had an accident. He had slept badly and was tired. When he was clambering up a steep hill, which was covered with a mass of slippery stones, he slipped and nearly fell. Mary cried out, but the donkey was just able to keep his balance and go on climbing. But his foot hurt. Mary and Joseph soon noticed that he was limping.

"You poor dear," Mary comforted him. "You have carried me now for such a long time. We'll soon be there, though and then you can have a rest."

The donkey trotted along as well as he could, although this was not so fast as usual. Joseph had no trouble in keeping up with him on this day. They reached Bethlehem in the afternoon. The town was surrounded by a wall, and travellers could only enter through a gate. A watchman sat in the gateway and Joseph had to tell him his name, Mary's name and where they came from and what their business was before he let them through.

Then at last they were in Bethlehem.

"Oh Joseph, how happy I am," Mary said. "The Lord be praised, that we have reached this place. And thank you, my dear little donkey. It has been hard and difficult for you, but you were so good."

"He's worth his weight in gold," said Joseph, feeling very glad. "We should never have made it without him."

The donkey felt so proud and happy.

"Hee-haw!" he cried, and looked round for the birds of Nazareth.

They were all sitting in a row on the town wall.

"You have done very well, little donkey," they chirped.

The stable

Joseph and Mary soon discovered that Bethlehem was a town with houses as small and streets as narrow as Nazareth. But which way should they go to find lodgings?

They set off at random and soon came to an inn. "They rent rooms here to travellers," explained Joseph. "Wait, I'll ask them if we can stay here."

But when he went in he found that every room was occupied. Not even the smallest corner was free. It was too full.

"We must go to the next inn," Joseph said to Mary. "There are several, for sure."

They went on looking in one narrow street after another.

"My wife is tired, and her child may be born at any moment," Joseph said each time he came to an inn.

And all the landlords gave the same answer: "Impossible. Try somewhere else."

When they had tried everywhere Joseph suggested, "Perhaps a family will take us in."

"I am worried most about our little donkey," Mary sighed. "Look, how badly he is limping! He must have a good rest."

"Let's try this house," Joseph said and he knocked.

"Kind friend, can you put us up for the night," Joseph asked. "We have only just arrived in Bethlehem, but there is no room for us in any inn."

"I am sorry," the old man assured them. "You

would have been welcome to stay here, but a family with children came here just before you came, and I have taken them in. I haven't the smallest corner free now. But try my neighbour. He has a good heart."

"Thank you for your friendliness," Joseph said, and he knocked at the next house.

Here he met with the same answer, and at the house after that, and so on right to the end of the street. Too many people had come to Bethlehem at the command of mighty Caesar.

"If the donkey could still manage, I think it would be best to go back to the shepherds," Joseph finally decided. "But I don't know if he could find the way in the dark."

"God will certainly help us," Mary said to comfort him. "Be calm, Joseph. The donkey has found somewhere for us to stay every time."

"I hope you are right, Mary," Joseph replied, "but the donkey has changed."

Yes, the donkey was quite different from his usual self. He had severe pain in his leg, and he was dog-tired. He let his head hang down almost to the ground. That is why he did not see the angel.

But the angel knew what to do. When the donkey failed to look up, he waved to the birds of Nazareth. They came immediately. They had watched the donkey, Joseph and Mary wandering hither and thither through Bethlehem all the afternoon, and they were very worried. Now they were happy again! Suddenly the donkey pricked his ears. What sort of birds were these chirping away so loud and clear in the cold and dark?

Of course, they were the birds of Nazareth. And what were they singing?

"Come, come, come, little donkey! Here there is warmth and shelter."

At that he stretched his neck and lifted up his head.

He saw the angel at the end of a side street. Without limping, he stepped out eagerly in his direction.

"Do you hear that, Joseph," Mary asked in surprise. "My birds are singing."

"I do," Joseph said. "It's strange. I have never heard the chirping of birds in the middle of the night before, let alone in such a cold one."

"The donkey has found the way," smiled Mary. "He is in a hurry suddenly."

Now the donkey broke into a real trot and Joseph had to run to keep up. He did this gladly enough.

The thick clouds which had darkened the sky over Bethlehem all the afternoon and evening suddenly vanished at this moment, and it became clear.

A big star was shining exactly over the town, a star which no one had seen before. When the donkey rounded the next corner they approached a house, which was gleaming and white. At the door an angel beckoned and smiled, while in the garden the birds of Nazareth were chirping. Joseph and Mary heard the birds singing and saw the house but the angel they could not see.

"What kind of a palace is that?" asked the astonished Joseph. "It is glittering all over. What can it be built with? It must be the house of a very rich man."

"We can't go in there," Mary said anxiously. "Not simple people like us. But Joseph, it seems that the donkey led us here on purpose."

Joseph tried to hold the donkey back, but the donkey was very obstinate.

"Joseph dear," said Mary, "perhaps it's all right after all, my birds are singing in the garden."

"Are they really and truly?" Joseph asked in astonishment.

But when they came nearer to the house Joseph and Mary saw that it wasn't wealthy and big at all, as they had first thought. It was a plain, old stable with twisty walls. The radiant starlight had made it appear brilliantly white and splendid.

"Oh!" Mary cried in delight. "Only a stable! This is where we are to live all right. I would never have expected to stay in some fine house. We are much too dirty and covered with dust."

"Good," said Joseph and heaved a sigh of relief. "We'll stay here. That suits me. I'll ask the old man at the door."

There really was an old, stooping man standing in front of the house. He had heard the unusual bird song in the dark night, and had gone out to look at these birds. Then he noticed the star with its bright light. But because he was standing in front of the stable he did not notice that the star was making it shine like silver. He saw the donkey coming along the road with Mary and Joseph. The light of the star fell on them with such brilliance that the old man believed that a king and queen were approaching him.

"There comes the king I have dreamt about," he thought. "And his queen is with him too. What beautiful clothes they are wearing, as if they were woven from silver threads. And whoever saw such a donkey! He is as glossy as the finest silk and his hoofs gleam like pure gold. How can I find the courage to ask them into my house?"

The old man began to tremble with excitement as the travellers drew near. But these people were poor. A quite ordinary donkey was carrying a poor young woman on his back, and the man who was leading the donkey had simple and dusty clothes.

While the old man was standing and blinking in astonishment Joseph bowed deeply and said: "Good friend, give us shelter for tonight. We are all very tired. My wife and the donkey must have rest."

The old man opened the door. "I only have this old stable. There is room enough in it along with my two sheep and my cow. If you are prepared to be satisfied with it."

"Of course we shall be content with it," Joseph said. "Nothing would please us more."

"It is strange," the old man told them. "Last night in a dream I was ordered to clean and tidy my stable and to bring all my hay in from the field. A king would come to visit. And when I woke, I carried all these orders out, although I laughed at myself for doing so. What would a king want with my stable? What would he want hay for? And then you came along the road, and everything gleamed so brilliantly as though you really were King Solomon and the Queen of Sheba. In fact, you are poor travellers. I prefer that; I would have been shy before a king. But I am standing here talking. Come in! Enter!"

"Do you know, old man," said Mary, "at first we thought that your house was a shining palace. But then we realized that the bright star had made it look like silver."

"A remarkable evening," the old man said. "This great star, which has not been seen before, and bird song in the middle of a winter's night. This is what made me come out."

"Those are my birds," Mary explained. "They have flown after us all the way from Nazareth. I am sure they were calling the donkey, to help us find our way."

"God's ways are strange," the old man said. "Would you like to share my simple supper and then rest? What a good thing that I brought all my hay home today. You will be able to lie on it."

"We are really comfortable here," Mary said.

"No king and no queen could have anything better," Joseph laughed.

But the little donkey was already asleep in a corner.

He had carried Mary to her destination. At last he could sleep.

The child

The little donkey was dreaming. He dreamt that he was back home in Nazareth and grazing in Mary's meadow. It was early in springtime and all ground everything was in blossom, and green and fragrant. The birds were singing and flying hither and thither in sheer delight. He heard someone crying and suddenly knew that the birds were rejoicing over Mary's child. His heart thumped with joy. "The child is born now." thought the donkey in his dream.

Even the sun wanted to do something and shone so dazzlingly bright in his eyes that it woke him. "Oh, it was only a dream," thought the disappointed donkey.

It wasn't spring, and not even Nazareth, but the old, tumbledown stable in Bethlehem.

But — there was the scent of spring flowers — and there was singing — and everything was dazzlingly bright. The donkey opened his eyes and looked around him.

In a corner of the stable Mary was sitting and in a circle round her was a throng of angels, and they were singing.

The angels pressed closer and closer to Mary and even touched her with their wings. What were they trying to see? A warm feeling came over the donkey.

Suddenly an angel moved so far to one side that the donkey had a clear view. Oh, Mary was fondling a tiny baby!

So now it really had been born!

Joseph had opened the baggage and spread the lovely baby clothes which Mary had sewn. The angels

passed them to Mary and Mary wrapped the baby up
fine and warm in them. Then she lifted the little one
up so that all could see him and then handed him to
Joseph. Joseph put him down on the hay in a manger.
Thereupon all the angels stood round the manger and
sang. They sang very beautifully and so softly that
they could scarcely be heard.

Joseph and the owner of the stable listened peacefully and quietly to the angels and gazed at the child.
By chance Mary looked across towards the donkey
and noticed how he was craning his neck.

"Oh, Joseph," she said, "show him to our little
donkey."

74

Joseph led the donkey to the manger. There the donkey smelt that the hay had the fragrance of spring flowers.

Suddenly it was dark in the stable. The angels had all disappeared.

But through a gap in the roof the star shone down right on to the manger while everything else was in darkness. The donkey saw quite clearly how around the child there was radiant light. Joseph and the old man saw this too.

"The star's light is so bright," the old man said, "that it places the child on a throne. Now I begin to understand why I dreamt that a king would come here."

The little child lay there with his large, dark eyes open. The donkey tried to sniff and smell him a little. What cheeks he had, how warm and soft they were! He had eyes like an angel.

The old man said, "Mary, look how bright your baby's eyes are! Like bright stars! You could believe that the glory of the kingdom of heaven is reflected in them. I ask myself what kind of child this can be."

He was soon to learn the answer.

There was a knock at the door. The old man went and opened the door. Outside were standing the shepherds with whom Joseph and Mary had spent the previous night. The donkey immediately recognized Reuben.

"Is there a newly born child here?" a shepherd asked.

"A child wrapped in swaddling clothes and lying in a manger?" cried a clear, eager voice.

"Yes," replied the old man. "Come in. But please be quiet."

The shepherds walked across the stable and approached the manger on tiptoe.

In front of the manger they fell to their knees. For

a long while they did not move. Reuben's eyes were very bright and his old grandfather was wiping tears away. The donkey heard angels singing outside.

The shepherds stood up again slowly and hesitatingly, as though they would gladly have knelt and prayed longer.

"Where are the child's parents?" the grandfather asked. "We have a wonderful story to tell them."

When the shepherds saw Joseph and Mary they were very surprised.

"It's you?" they said. "We expected to find rich people. But God knows best."

Then the old shepherd began to tell their story. "We were keeping watch over our flocks as usual. The night was unusually clear because of the light of a big star which had not been seen before. Suddenly an angel of the Lord appeared to us, and we were filled with fear. And the angel said to us: 'Be not afraid; for behold I bring you good news of a great joy, which will come to all the people; for to you is born this day in the city of David a Saviour, who is Christ the Lord. And this will be a sign for you: you will find a child wrapped in swaddling cloths and lying in a manger.'

"And suddenly we saw all the sky was full of angels singing: 'The glory of God in the highest
    and peace on earth to men of goodwill'.

"Then the angels went away and we said to one another, 'Let us go over to Bethlehem and see this child of whom the angels spoke.' Hurriedly we set out."

"But how could you find your way here?" asked the old man, puzzled.

"That was not difficult," a shepherd answered. "At first we went along the usual road to Bethlehem. Then we saw the star shining over this house while all the others were in darkness. We knew that it was the glory of God being poured over the house."

"My stable!" the old man said.

For some time it was quiet then. The shepherds stood and gazed at the child. It was difficult for them to tear themselves away.

"If only I could stay with you and the little child," Reuben sighed as he stroked the little donkey.

"So I was allowed to learn what sort of a child this is," the old man reflected. "Just think of it! The Saviour in my stable!"

"The Good Shepherd," Reuben said, smiling blissfully.

"Truly, God has given us great joy," his grandfather said. "Now we must go back to our flocks. It is time to drive the animals out to pasture."

The shepherds left. Day began to break. The star grew pale. The little child, Mary and Joseph were asleep. But the donkey continued to stand by the manger. Joseph had forgotten to lead him back to his stall. He was standing quite still, guarding the little child.

He thought of his friends back home in Nazareth. The donkey knew that it would be quite a long time before Mary could travel home with the child. Joseph had said so the day before. Too many people had come to Bethlehem to have their names written.

With all his heart the donkey wanted the animals at home to have some message about the child.

"What a pity," he thought. "Here the dearest child in the world is lying. He has eyes which reflect the glory of God. And the sheep, the goats and their young ones don't know it. I know they are all waiting so impatiently. How can I send a message?"

While the donkey stood and racked his brains the sun rose. The birds of Nazareth in the trees round the stable woke up and began to sing their song of rejoicing. One of them peeped through a hole in the roof.

"Donkey!" he whispered. "May we see the child? We saw and heard the angels in the night and knew that the child had been born. But we didn't dare sing with the angels. May we come in now?"

Already a sparrow had flown through the hole. It was the little bird who always hopped sideways. He perched quickly on the edge of the manger.

"Psst!" hissed the donkey.

But when the bird saw the child he just couldn't keep still. He gave a tiny "peep". This was too much for his comrades outside. They pushed through the hole in the roof and soon the whole flock was in the stable. They perched wherever they could find room, close, very close to the manger! One or two even perched on the sleeping Mary, and a whole crowd of them on the donkey.

"Psst! You must be quiet! Psst!" the donkey warned them. "You may look, but you must keep still, or you'll wake him."

For a moment the birds really were as quiet as mice. When the boldest of them, though, could wait no longer and perched on the baby's hand, three others hurriedly flew across and chased him away.

"You must behave," whispered the donkey. "Otherwise you can't stay here." Now the child moved his tiny hand in his sleep. This was too much for the birds. They sang their song of exultation. Oh, how they trilled, and chirped and sang!

Mary woke and smiled and then Joseph woke. He too had to laugh.

The old man said that nothing could ever surprise him after this.

Finally the baby woke too. The birds were silent now, ashamed and anxious because they had woken him. Only the boldest bird dared to fly down onto the manger and show off his skill.

"My little birds," Mary said. "Thank you for your

song. Now you have seen my child. Wouldn't the best thing now be to fly back home. I am sure it is very empty in Nazareth without you."

Now the little donkey realized how he could send a message.

"My dear birds," he said. "Do what Mary says and fly home. And tell everyone — especially the lambs and the little goats — what has happened here."

"We still want to sing a cradle song for the little child," they begged. "May we?"

And they sang so beautifully and so softly that the little boy closed his eyes again and went on sleeping.

Then the birds flew away, through the hole in the roof. They chirped good-bye and disappeared, heading north, towards Nazareth.

"How lucky you are, being able to go home," the donkey thought. "I am homesick for Nazareth too. All the same I am luckier than all the others, for I can stay with the child and with Mary and Joseph, and be their little donkey."

Bethlehem

Mary's little donkey was tethered outside the old stable.

"We've been here in Bethlehem a long time now," he was thinking as he munched some fresh hay. "I'm longing to get back home to Nazareth. I can just imagine how Mary's lambs and kids are waiting for us. 'Won't they be coming soon, mother?' they'll be crying, and stamping their feet impatiently."

The donkey laughed to himself as he thought of his little playmates at home.

"But soon we'll be going. I heard Joseph saying to Mary today: 'There are only a few families left to be enrolled,' and Mary said: 'Dear Joseph, why must we wait to be the last?' Then Joseph answered: 'They all say they are in a hurry,' and Mary sighed: 'Of course we are well housed here, but I do long for our own little home. 'I'm always thinking of our animals back there.' — 'Don't fret, Mary,' said Joseph, 'in a couple of days we'll be on our way home'."

And the little donkey gave a happy little whinny.

"Hee-haw," he said cautiously in case Mary's baby was asleep in the stable, for he did not want to wake him. And that made him think of the baby: "He is so soft and tender. And his eyes shine just like the good spring sunshine after the long winter, and no other child in all the world has eyes like his. That's what all the shepherds said. And the old man in the stable too.

And his black cow and the nice kind sheep think so too."

And when the donkey thought about the child he had to say "hee-haw" again.

"What are you laughing about, little donkey?" asked the sheep who was cropping the bit of grass by the stable wall.

"Oh, I'm just thinking about Mary's baby," said the donkey. "It's the loveliest baby in all the world, and the nicest and cleverest and sweetest and . . ."

"Rarest and finest," put in the sheep, who did not think the donkey was overdoing it. "Have you ever thought how lovely it sounds when the baby laughs?"

"Yes, I think it sounds just like angels singing! Remember how they sang the night he was born."

The sheep turned the idea over in her mind. "Mm, perhaps you're right, but I rather think it sounds more like when it's raining."

"When it's raining!" cried the donkey, astonished.

"Yes when the rain-drops tinkle in the rain-barrel. Or like little bells."

"Angels singing," said the donkey firmly.

The black cow, who was taking a nap, opened her eyes and said:

"A little while ago I heard Mary saying to my master that you would be going home soon. Is that true, little donkey?"

"Yes certainly," replied the donkey, flicking his tail happily.

"Can't you stay a bit longer?" begged the sheep. "Till the baby can walk. I think it would be such fun to see him running about. Or wait at least till he can crawl."

"No, that's impossible," explained the donkey. "Mary has her animals who are waiting, and Joseph has his work."

"How I wanted to hear the boy talk," sighed the

cow. "I'm sure he will only learn gentle and good words."

"Yes, I'm sure of that," agreed the donkey.

"Can't you stay till he begins to talk?" asked the cow. "That won't be so long now."

"No," answered the donkey. "We're leaving this week."

The cow and the sheep were sad, but the donkey lifted up his head happily and looked at the sky.

"Oh look! What a beautiful star!" he said. The other two looked up. The sun had just set and the darkness was sweeping in. The great star shone more and more clearly.

"Ah ha," said the donkey, "now I recognize it, it is the very same star that shone over the stable when we came here. It shone just as clear and bright that night when the child was born."

"I wonder what's going to happen tonight," the sheep murmured. "Perhaps the angels are coming here again."

"Who knows!" said the cow.

The strangers

Mary and Joseph came out.

"How wonderful it is tonight," said Mary. "So quiet. And so light."

"As if it were some festival," added Joseph.

The old man stuck his head out.

"Hey, what's that shining there?" he said.

"I recognize it again now," cried Mary in some surprise. "It's the very same star that brought us here the night the child was to be born. Oh I wonder what is going to happen tonight."

"Oh yes, that was the night you came," recalled the old man. "Over there at the bend in the road I saw you, and I thought it was a king and queen coming."

"And it was only us poor folk. But look, there *is* someone coming," said Mary.

"Tonight it really is grand folk who are travelling," exclaimed Joseph, amazed. "Look what huge camels they have. They're shining like silver."

"And what noble riders they are!" cried Mary. "Joseph, they're coming here. How strange!"

"No stranger than your own coming," said the stable-man. "Nothing can surprise me any more."

The travellers now drew level with the stable, and now you could see clearly how grand they were. Their camels were very, very beautiful and they had saddles and bridles studded with gold and precious stones which shone and sparkled in the starlight when the foremost camel shook its head.

And what fine riders they were. In their rich clothes they looked like princes.

"We are seeking the new-born King of the Jews," said the first.

"We have seen his star in the East, and it has led us to this house," said the second.

"We have come to worship the Light of the World," said the third.

Joseph was so surprised he could not speak. He looked round for Mary, but she had gone in to the child.

The three travellers were still quite sure that they had come to the right place, for they beckoned to their servants to help them dismount.

Now Joseph noticed that there were several smaller camels behind the three bigger ones. Their riders jumped quickly from their saddles and hurried forward to help their lords.

Tall and stately was the first stranger as he stood upon the ground. He stretched forth his arms towards the star. Then he looked like a giant, thought Joseph — like a young champion.

"Now," the stranger asked in his deep voice, "Where is the Child-King?"

Joseph did not know what to answer, but just then a happy baby-voice came from inside the stable.

"In there!" cried the second traveller. He was not so stately as his gigantic friend. But he had keen eyes and such an air of authority that Joseph guessed he was a man who ruled over many people. But even he had to bend his proud neck when he entered the stable.

The third stranger, however, had to be lifted down from his camel. He was very old and thin and bent, and he leaned heavily on his stick when he walked.

It was dark in the stable, but through a gap in the roof the starlight shone on to the crib, and it gleamed and glimmered all round the babe lying on the straw, smiling and waving to the newcomers.

"Is it the star that is shining so, or does the light come from the child?" the strangers wondered as they bowed themselves to the ground before the little one. Then the babe began to chuckle contentedly, filling the little stable with his merry crowing so that the dignified lords had to smile.

The strong warrior bent his knee. The babe started to struggle as hard as he could so as to get to him. Mary lifted up the child and laid him in the strong man's arms.

"O thou king of all the earth," whispered the man, "I am the strongest of men, but I am as weak as a babe when I hold thee in mine arms, for thou art stronger than I."

Humbly he kissed the little fingers and handed the babe to the second traveller, the proud ruler with the keen eyes.

"Oh, now I may hold thee in my arms," said he softly. "Thou who shalt be ruler of all the world. I am rich and mighty, and men obey the least wave of my hand, but beside thee I am poor and mean, for thou art mightier than I."

Very carefully he kissed the boy's hair and laid him in the arms of the third, the aged stranger who trembled so much that he could hardly hold the babe, yet allowed no one to help him.

"Thou child, thou child," he whispered, "Thou art come at last, thou for whom the world has waited so long. I possess all wisdom and knowledge but when I hold thee in mine arms I admit that I know less than a child, for thou art wiser than I."

The babe laughed and tugged hard at the old man's long white beard. Mary had to hasten forward and unclasp the strong little fingers. The old man kissed the child's forehead and smiled. Then he drew forth

a soft leather pouch and poured out some coarse
brown grains into a bowl. He lit them with an ember
from the fire and the low room was filled with billowing
fragrant smoke.

Joseph and Mary watched him in wonder. Then he
spoke: "We three have come a long way from the
lands of Orient to worship a king. Now we are burning
incense in his honour after the custom of our country."

The princely stranger opened a casket and brought
forth ashes with myrrh which also had a wonderful
scent. But he did not have to light the myrrh for it was
fragrant already.

86

"The most precious thing which I possess is myrrh," he said. "That is what we give to kings in our country."

The young and stately warrior stood by the crib and played with the child, who touched his priceless ring and tried to take hold of the enormous shining pearl. The man took off his ring and laid it in the child's hand.

"Royal Child," said he, "thou shalt have the ring of truth, for it is the most precious thing that I have."

Whereupon he took gold coins and offered them to Joseph.

"See, here is gold for the babe," said he.

"Such a little child should not receive such great gifts," protested Mary.

But the old stranger said, "We saw his star when first it shone, one night some moons ago. We knew then that at that hour a great king was born, and we resolved to make the journey to behold him."

And the younger went on: "Truly, we have come to worship a king, and so our gifts must be royal."

Mary answered, "Indeed you are right. He shall become a king, for the angels foretold it."

Then the strangers wanted to hear more. Mary told them how the Angel Gabriel had come to her in Nazareth and told her that she should bear a child who should be the world's Redeemer and King.

They all listened in silence. Then the old man said, "Wonderful are the ways of God."

"He has brought us here in a wonderful way," said the two others.

Meanwhile the slaves were crowding into the doorway. They were curious about the child who had caused their masters to come all the way to the Land of Judah. They craned their necks to catch a glimpse of him. Mary noticed them.

"Come in, come in," she said, making room for them round the crib.

"But what is it that is shining so brightly?" whispered the slaves. "Is the light coming from the child's eyes, or is it the star shining in?"

"This babe shall some time be King of the World," said the old man.

The slaves fell on their knees and touched the ground with their foreheads. But the child smiled just as happily to them as to their royal masters.

"May you always be as mild as you are now," said one of the slaves. "You shall come to rule the earth with the sceptre of goodness and it shall be good to live in your kingdom even as poor servants."

The babe nodded his head and looked very earnest for a moment.

"It is just as if he understands," said the slave amazed.

Mary took the child and laid him in the slave's arms.

"Yes, he shall become a king," she said softly. "But he shall also be the World's Redeemer and then he must be everyone's servant, even the servant of slaves."

"O King of kings who shall be the servant of servants," whispered the slave. "How good is God to send you to the poor on earth!"

Mary laid the baby in the crib and he went to sleep at once. The others stood looking at him in silence for a while, the grand lords and the poor servants, then the stately stranger spoke: "Set up the tents for the night. It is time to rest. Early tomorrow morning we must start on our journey back."

"The journey has taken a long time," he told Joseph later, "and on our return we must visit King Herod in Jerusalem. On our way here we went to his palace to ask about the new-born King of the Jews. But King Herod had not even heard about him. He was very happy when he heard what we had to tell. And he asked us to return and tell him where the child was to be found, for he too wishes to come and worship him."

A cold gust of wind blew through the night and the light of the star sank down. Mary shivered and wrapped her shawl round the child. She knew, and Joseph knew, and their host knew that Herod was a very wicked king and they could not believe that he could wish the child any good. But they hardly dared say that to their noble guests.

"Joseph, I am so uneasy," whispered Mary after the strangers had gone to their tents. "I fear King Herod so. Supposing he were to come here!"

"We must try and get away from here as soon as possible," answered Joseph. "Bethlehem is too close to Jerusalem. We'll be safer at home in Nazareth. I shall be ready tomorrow or the day after, I'm sure, and then we'll be off."

"Oh how I wish the good men wouldn't have to tell King Herod where the child is," said Mary. "Can't we ask them not to, Joseph?"

"I hardly dare speak to such grand folk," replied Joseph uneasily.

"Dear Joseph, you must . . . for the child's sake," begged Mary.

"Yes, I'll try tomorrow before we set off," Joseph promised.

The camels were lying outside the stable. The donkey was tethered to the door. The spring night was mild and smelled beautifully of fresh grass and flowers.

"Little donkey," said one of the camels, "why do your grand owners live in such a tumbledown old stable?"

"Joseph is a poor man," answered the donkey. "He's not grand at all."

"Where does he keep his flocks and herds?" asked another camel.

"Flocks and herds!" cried the donkey. "*I'm* his flocks and herds, that's all he has. Of course at home in Nazareth Mary has a few sheep and goats."

"Do you mean to say that it's a poor man that you work for?" puzzled the camel. "Why then have our rich masters come all the way here to visit him?"

"That I don't know," replied the donkey. "But would I be any happier with a master rich in money? Mary and Joseph are rich in goodness and kindness and helpfulness. I must say that it is wonderful to have a master who never beats me or shouts or wants to make me carry more than I can manage."

"You're right there," agreed the camel, "We animals think more of a good man than of a rich one. But tell me, little donkey, what's so special about the child in there. I heard our masters talking about him during the journey. They've hardly spoken about anything else. Who is he?"

"He is the Good Shepherd," said the donkey quietly.

"The Good Shepherd!" cried the camel.

"The Good Shepherd!" echoed the other animals. "Is that the truth?"

"The angels sang about him all night long when he was born. He is the Redeemer of the whole world, and its King and Shepherd," said the cow proudly.

Then the camels lifted up their heads to the clear spring sky. For the rest of the night they were silent thinking over what they had been told. When at last day was breaking the donkey spoke: "On your way home if you pass through a town called Nazareth please will you greet all the animals there and tell them that all's well with the child and Mary and Joseph. And tell them we're coming home soon, because that's where we come from."

"We've never heard of such a town," answered the

camels, "but if we do go that way we won't forget. But now we have a request to make to you."

"What is it?" asked the donkey.

"We want to see the child before we go home. Can you help us?"

"I'll try," the donkey promised.

In the morning, as they were coming out of their tents the tall warrior said: "Last night I dreamed that an angel came and commanded me to go back home another way and not to go to Jerusalem and speak with the King."

"Strange!" cried his companion. "That is exactly what I dreamed."

At that moment the old stranger came slowly towards them. "I was told by angels in a dream that we should return by another way," he said.

"Why, that is what we two have also dreamt. We should obey."

So they decided to go straight home. Joseph was pleased when he heard that!

"It was surely God who sent the dreams to the strangers," he thought. "For he knows how shy I am. He saw that I did not dare to speak with them. That *was* good of him!"

"Now perhaps you will pass through Nazareth," said the donkey to the camels, "and greet the animals there."

"We shall do that for you," said the camels, "but you must keep your promise too."

Then the donkey started to bray and scrape the door with his hoof until Mary came out.

"Wait a bit, my little donkey," she said. "I'll come and give you your water soon."

And so she went in again.

"Oh dear," said the camels disappointed.

"We'll just wait a little," said the donkey cheerfully. "She hasn't got the baby up yet."

The animals waited impatiently while the servants saddled them, and then they heard the baby wake inside the stable.

"Now!" said the donkey, and he brayed and pawed the ground till at last Mary came out, and there she had the child in her arms.

"Ooh!" said all the camels.

The slaves forgot what they were about as they came to look at the little one.

"What's the matter with you today?" said Mary to her donkey.

But he kept on shaking his head and pawing the ground so that Mary went up to him.

"Are you ill?" she wondered. "You don't usually make all this fuss!"

The donkey laid his head on Mary's shoulder.

"Oh, you just want to say good morning, you little rascal," said Mary, laughing. "Well, you can do that."

The camels craned their heads forward to her, and she lifted up the child quite close to them before she went in again.

"You did that well, little donkey," said the camels, "so thank you very much, for we'll never forget that you let us see the Good Shepherd."

The dream

The little donkey woke up with a start. His heart was beating and he found that he was strangely frightened. At the same time he heard the child stir in the crib.

"Ah, there he is after all," he thought thankfully. "All's well. It was just a dream. It's terrible what you can dream."

And what a dream he had had! He had dreamt that they had come home to Nazareth and all Mary's animals had come rushing up to welcome them.

"May we see the child? May we see the child?" cried all the little kids and lambs, skipping with excitement. "Where have you got the child?"

It was then that the donkey noticed that the child was not with them. Nor was Mary. Nobody was riding on his back, only a big heavy bundle.

"But what have you done with the child?" asked the oldest sheep.

"He was there just now," puzzled the donkey.

"But where is he now, and where's Mary?"

Indeed where *was* the baby, and where *was* Mary?" The donkey was terribly worried.

"Did you leave them in the wilderness and a lion has eaten them up?" asked the goats.

"Did they slip off your back over the cliffs and on to the rocks below?" suggested the sheep.

"Did you lose them in the river when you crossed it?" cried the lambs.

But the donkey could not remember anything like that. Only that he had been hurrying up the hill to Nazareth to show the child to his friends.

"And we've been so longing to see him," wailed the little lambs and the kids.

The donkey felt his heart tighten with fright. It was then that he had woken up and found that it was only a dream, and he was standing in the dark in the stable in Bethlehem; Mary, Joseph and the old man were asleep on the straw on the floor and the child was lying in the crib.

"Oh, how we've been longing . . ." The donkey heard like an echo from his dream.

"That was because Joseph and Mary were talking so much about the journey home yesterday evening," he thought.

Joseph had said that everything was done now and they could go home.

"Oh, how I've been longing," said Mary. "We've been here nearly three months now, and the baby's getting quite big."

"Yes, he'll manage the journey home fine," said Joseph.

"And the spring sunshine is so bright and warm. Everything is so beautiful that you might think we were walking in God's meadows in paradise," said Mary. "Dear Joseph, what a lovely journey home it will be!"

"Yes it will be quite different from when we were coming here. It was winter then and cold. And how it rained! Do you remember?"

"But our good donkey helped us," said Mary. "Think how much it will mean to him to be going home. I've seen how homesick he is."

That was how they had been talking before they went to sleep, and it had made the donkey so happy. Fancy having such a horrible dream.

"But a dream is only a dream and it doesn't mean so very much," he thought.

Just then he noticed how it was growing light in the

94

stable. At first there was a faint gleam which gradually grew brighter. At last the donkey could make out clearly an angel in shining robes. The angel bent over Joseph and whispered: "Joseph, Joseph, hearken carefully!"

But Joseph tossed in his sleep and thrashed out with his arms as if he would chase away the angel that was disturbing his sleep.

"Joseph," said the angel, "you must arise at once. You must waken Mary. Gather together all that you have and take the child and flee, but not home. King Herod seeks to kill the child, and you must hide yourselves in Egypt for a time. Be not afraid. The angels shall protect you. Hearken Joseph, wake up now! There is no time to lose!"

Joseph stirred, mumbled and opened his eyes.

The angel stroked the donkey's muzzle and that was like the softest breath of the west wind.

"Mary's little donkey," whispered the angel, "you must help me to take the child to safety."

Then the angel vanished.

"What on earth have I dreamt?" wondered Joseph. "That I must flee into Egypt with the child! What an idea! No, no, tomorrow we're all set to go home to Nazareth. That'll be good." Joseph wanted to snuggle down and sleep again.

But the donkey stamped and neighed so that Joseph became wide awake and got up.

"What's the matter?" he asked.

The donkey brayed so that it echoed through the little stable. Oh, he made it sound as if it was most urgent. Mary woke up, and the old man woke up.

"What is it?" asked Mary. "I feel so afraid. There's no danger about."

"It was only the donkey that frightened you. Lie down and sleep a bit longer."

"No," said Mary, "there's something. He doesn't bray like that for nothing."

"Well," said Joseph thoughtfully, "I did have a strange dream. An angel came to me and said we should journey to Egypt at once and stay there for a time because King Herod wants to kill our child."

"Oh," said Mary shivering, "I am so afraid of him. We must flee. At once. Now in the night."

"But Mary, it was only a dream. Sleep now. Tomorrow we can think it over."

But the donkey brayed again.

"No," said Mary, "I believe that the donkey has

seen the angel and knows that he really did speak to you. You can see by the donkey that there is danger threatening. Let's flee at once, Joseph."

Then Joseph realized that the angel really had warned him in the dream. He helped Mary to pack and load up the donkey. It was still dark but he fanned the embers on the hearth so that they could see.

The old man who looked after the stable was sad.

"Must you go so soon?" he asked. "Right in the middle of the night! Wait till morning at least."

"We must hurry," said Joseph, "the child is in danger."

"Oh, you know, no one's going to harm a little child. It's just a bad dream you've had."

"But the angel I saw in my dream told me to leave at once," answered Joseph, "and our donkey also saw the angel."

"Wait till it gets light anyway," begged the old man. "There are still some wild animals about, and they could kill you and the baby."

"We are not afraid of wild animals," said Joseph. "It's not them that are after the child's life."

"Who is it then?" asked the old man, smiling.

"King Herod!"

"Yes, but the strangers from the East didn't go to see him on their way back after all. He can't know yet where the baby is," objected the old man.

"Somehow he's found out," said Joseph. "And he wants to kill the child because he can't bear that goodness and justice should have any power here on earth."

"Well, do as you think best," said the old man, "and may the Lord preserve you."

"We are very grateful to you for giving us lodging all this time," said Joseph. "See here is a yoke which I've made for you from an olive root I found in a crevice."

97

"That *is* well made," said the old man, "Thank you very much. My old yoke was falling to bits and couldn't be mended."

"Yes I saw you needed a new one," said Joseph smiling.

Mary took the old man's hand and said, "Here I have sewn a cloak for you from the cloth I got from the men of the East."

"Oh it's so warm and soft! It's much too fine for me, but I *do* like it. My cloak is quite worn out."

"I saw that you needed one," said Mary. "Isn't it lucky I got it ready in time."

"Now that you're going," said the man, "I'd like to thank you for honouring my lowly stable by coming here so that the Redeemer of the World might be born in it. No place on earth will be counted so great and holy as this little hut."

By now the donkey was getting restless. How much longer were they going to stand around saying good-bye? Hadn't the angel said there was no time to be lost? He pawed the ground and butted Joseph in the back.

"Yes, yes," said Joseph, "we must hurry."

Mary went into the stable. The child was still sleeping in the crib and smiled in his sleep as Mary lifted him up.

Mary wrapped the baby in a shawl and handed him to the old man who carried him out to the donkey. Joseph lifted Mary on to the donkey's back. The old man kissed the child's cheek and handed him back to his mother.

The donkey trotted off right away at full speed. Joseph had to run to keep up with him.

It was still dark, but the donkey could see quite well in the dark and soon found a little path that led out on to the high road.

"It's just as well," said Mary thoughtfully, "that we

didn't get in at one of the inns inside the walls. We shouldn't have been able to get out of the town before the gates were opened in the morning. And maybe even then, it would have been too late."

"Yes, it was good that we were staying out here," said Joseph. "Now the roads are open." Suddenly he called out:

"Wait! My cloak has got caught in a bush."

Mary reined in the donkey while Joseph freed himself.

"It's so quiet," said Mary. "Look, it's growing light in the east. Soon the sun will be up."

The donkey pricked up his ears. He had heard hoof beats far off.

Now Joseph could hear them too.

"It's some horsemen," he said. "Who could be out so early?"

The hoof-beats came nearer and nearer.

"We'll hide in the wood here," said Joseph taking the donkey's bridle.

No sooner were they in the wood than a troop of soldiers rode by in a great hurry without seeing Joseph and Mary. Just as they topped a rise in the direction of Bethlehem the sun rose and its first rays gleamed on their polished helmets.

"Oh," breathed Mary, "I'm glad we went out of their way."

"Yes indeed," said Joseph. "But now we must hasten on."

Neither Joseph nor Mary had any idea that the soldiers had been sent by King Herod to look for their child.

All day they journeyed south, never daring to stop. Towards evening they were very tired. The sun went down and it grew dark.

"It is rather eerie in the wilderness tonight," said Mary.

99

"We'll have to stay here all the same," said Joseph.

Mary slid down from the donkey. They ate some bread which the old man in the stable had given them, and the donkey chewed some hay which he had carried on his back.

Joseph and Mary lay down on the ground with their heads against the donkey's belly. The child stretched his hands towards the sky as if to play with the gleaming lights up there.

A great star fell and he cried out happily as it shot through space.

"The baby isn't afraid of the dark," said Joseph. "He feels just as safe out here as in the stable."

"Look how he reaches up with his arms to the stars," said Mary. "Look how they twinkle to him as if they were good friends."

Joseph and Mary became so interested in the child's playing that they quite forgot their fears and anxieties. The donkey began to snore softly and soon the baby fell asleep too. Even Joseph and Mary slept peacefully until it began to grow light again.

With the caravan

All the next day the little donkey trotted southwards carrying Mary and the child on his back. Joseph walked silently beside them.

There were fewer and fewer olive groves and vineyards now, and homes became more and more scattered, until finally they came to an end altogether. The country stretched out before the travellers, bare and empty. The sun blazed down, scorching hot. They had reached the great desert that separates the Land of Judah from Egypt. The donkey grew terribly tired from wading through the desert sands, and the fine dust got into his eyes and nostrils. But it was not only the donkey that found the going difficult, the sand was bothering Joseph and Mary too. Only the little child, who was asleep, well wrapped up in his mother's shawl, was untroubled.

"Oh how thirsty I am!" thought the donkey. "I have never been so thirsty. But if I push on hard, perhaps we'll reach Egypt tonight."

And so he tried to step out a bit in the heavy-going sand. Mary was looking forward to getting there too, for in the early afternoon she said:

"Joseph, do you think we'll get there today?"

But Joseph shook his head and said, "Dear Mary, they say it's a long way to Egypt. Many days' journey, I think. But don't worry, the angel promised to help us."

Mary sat silent for a while, but suddenly she called out: "I see buildings over there! And trees! It's the beginning of Egypt. Can't you see? Over there!"

Yes, far far away they could just see houses and some trees. The little donkey quickened his steps, quite excited. How lovely! Soon they would be there.

But it was only a stopping place for camel caravans at an oasis. There travellers could stay overnight. A large caravan had just arrived. A rich merchant had hired a whole caravan with camels and camel-drivers to carry his goods through the desert. The merchant himself was sitting at the table, and the host of the caravanserai stood beside him chatting as Mary and Joseph entered.

"It's not difficult for anyone with such a following as you have to journey through the desert," the host was saying. "But every day I see single families going past. They are fleeing from King Herod, but most of them end up in the sand and are never seen again. They are usually quite worn out when they get here, and even so they haven't really got into the desert yet."

Joseph and Mary looked at each other in alarm. Now they knew that their journey was going to be very difficult indeed.

"The angel will protect us," whispered Joseph and pressed Mary's hand.

Then the host noticed them.

"What do you want?" he asked roughly.

"Master, can you give us and our donkey lodging for the night?" answered Joseph.

"Can you pay?"

Joseph opened his purse and took out one of the gold pieces which the rich strangers had given to the child. At the same time the ring fell out by accident and rolled along the floor to the table where the merchant sat. The merchant was going to kick it away but he checked himself when he saw how a large pearl gleamed in the shadows.

Joseph bent down and picked up the ring.

"What a ring!" thought the merchant. "Never in my life have I seen one like it! I hardly believed such a pearl existed!"

"Where did you get that?" he asked, looking hard at Joseph. "You must be a thief. Why else are you out here in the desert?"

"The baby was given the ring by a very rich man," said Joseph calmly.

"The baby!" snorted the merchant. "People don't give rings to a baby! Confess! Where did you steal the ring and the gold coin from?"

"It's just as Joseph says," said Mary. "The baby got them both from some rich strangers."

The merchant looked closely at her. Strange! The poor woman met his gaze with such clear eyes that it was impossible that she should not be telling the truth, indeed impossible that she should be capable of even thinking up a lie. So he peeped at the child. There was nothing specially remarkable about the baby as he slept in his mother's arms. Whoever would give such a little tadpole costly presents?

"Hum," he said, "will you sell the ring?"

"No," said Joseph, "It belongs to the baby and he loves to play with it so much."

"These folk don't understand how valuable the ring is," thought the merchant. "Good! I'll get that ring! By hook or by crook!"

"Where are you going?" he asked in a rather more friendly tone.

"To Egypt," answered Joseph.

That pleased the merchant. No-one could travel through the desert with a little child on just a donkey. So he would invite these people to travel with his caravan and he would see to it that they would get well into debt with him for food and water. Then he would take the ring in payment when they arrived. Yes, that's what he would do!

"Listen now, my good man," he said, "You can't go travelling through the desert on a donkey. But I like you and I am a helpful sort of person: You can travel with my caravan and then you will come safely into Egypt."

Joseph bowed humbly and Mary smiled happily. "You are very good, master," said Joseph.

"God will reward you for your goodness," said Mary.

"Have you ever heard the like?" said the leader of the caravan when he came out to his men. "The merchant has allowed those poor folk with the donkey to travel with us to Egypt."

"What has he got in mind?" asked one of the men. "He's not doing that just to help them."

"He's got a heart of stone," said another.

"He has given them permission," said the leader, "and there's nothing we can do about it."

"Did you hear?" said one of the big beautiful camels when they were left alone, "we're going to have the company of a donkey through the desert."

"Ugh!" said another, turning up his mouth, "I don't fancy being in company of that sort!"

"How will a donkey keep up with us when we really get going?" asked a third.

"He'll collapse before we've got half way," said a fourth.

"That is the best that could happen," said the oldest camel, "then we shall arrive in Egypt without him and we won't be put to shame."

"Hush!" said the first, "here he comes."

"Look as if you don't see him!" said the oldest. "Don't speak to him, and don't answer if he says anything."

Joseph came leading the donkey and Mary followed right behind with the child.

The merchant came out and said, "You'll have to sell the donkey. You can't take him with you."

"Why not?" said Mary, taken aback.

"He can't keep up with the camels at the speed they go. But I'm sure the host will buy him for a good price, and then you can ride on my camels."

"We can't sell our donkey," said Joseph.

"He'll manage all right," said Mary.

"We'll be travelling through the desert for many days," said the merchant, "he'll never do it."

"God has given us the donkey," said Mary. "Without the donkey we should be lost, for he hears what we cannot hear and sees what we cannot see."

The merchant was annoyed. "What nonsense! Now be sensible, and sell him."

"Our donkey can see the good angels," said Joseph, "and he has always led us the right way. We are grateful that you wish to help us, but we cannot part with our donkey."

The merchant saw that he could not persuade them and so he went back in, muttering to himself.

"Don't be afraid, little donkey," said Joseph, "we won't sell you."

"Thank you, my own very special little donkey." Mary stroked his muzzle tenderly, "Thank you for bringing us to this good place."

By now the baby had woken up. When he saw all those splendid camels he began to wriggle and kick. He chuckled and smiled and stretched out his arms towards them as if to pat them all. Joseph laughed and lifted him up to the nearest one. That happened to be the oldest camel. The huge animal stayed quite still while the little one stroked it with his outstretched fingers.

Afterwards Mary went in with the child. Joseph took the baggage off the donkey's back and followed them in.

"Little donkey," said the oldest camel, who had quite forgotten that they were not going to talk to him, "who are those people, and who is the child?"

"Oh," said the donkey happily, "he is the one that's going to be the Good Shepherd!"

"The Good Shepherd!" echoed the camel. "You don't mean the one that God has promised to send to earth from heaven?"

"The very one!" said the donkey.

"Ah!" said all the animals, "the Good Shepherd."

"When he patted me I felt I could have run through the desert for days and nights, jumping and dancing."

"When he smiled," said the one next to him, "I could smell the most wonderful scent like newly mown hay and fresh flowers."

"The scent still lingers in the air," added another.

"Little donkey," said the old camel, "are you really meaning to carry the baby and his mother all through the desert right into Egypt? You'll never manage that."

"Oh yes, I will. I've already carried Mary all the way from Nazareth to Bethlehem."

"That's not very far. But it's a very, very long way to Egypt. I could carry him and his mother for you."

"No," said the donkey. "No one else is Mary's little donkey. Only me."

"Mm, but what if you get tired?"

"Well, we'll see," said the donkey. "Maybe you could take them now and again."

"Me too, me too," murmured the others.

"But is it true what your master says, that you have seen the angels?" asked another.

"Yes," replied the donkey, "every time there was any danger on the way an angel helped me. And he will do it again for so he has promised."

"But why are you going to Egypt?" asked the old camel.

"The wicked king wants to kill the child."

106

This news upset all the animals, they started to bawl and bellow and one of the camel-drivers came rushing out to see what was the matter. It took a long time before they were all quiet again.

Early next morning there was a lot of bustle in the caravanserai. Everything was ready for the departure, only the rich merchant was still at table, eating. Joseph had made the donkey's loads fast. Mary had got the little one ready and was sitting on the donkey's back playing with the child. The camels craned their long necks to see him laughing, quite forgetting their usual proud ways.

Suddenly a noise of horses' hooves was heard and very soon a troop of soldiers appeared.

"Mary," cried Joseph alarmed, "Soldiers are coming! Perhaps they're looking for us! Where can we hide?"

At once all the camels crowded round the donkey and hid him and Mary from the soldiers' view.

The leading horseman slid quickly from his horse and called out: "Have you seen a young couple with a baby?"

"Who would go off into the desert with a baby?" said the merchant. "What would they do there?"

"They could try and hide the child."

"Why?"

"The king has found out that a child was born in Bethlehem recently, and it is foretold that that child will become king one day. And King Herod means to put a stop to that."

"Well, why don't you look in Bethlehem?"

"We've ransacked the whole town. But King Herod got to hear that a young couple who were living in a stable outside the town had disappeared with their little child the very night we went there."

"Bah! A royal child doesn't live in a stable," said

the merchant, "and you won't find him out here in the desert! Look in the villages round Bethlehem! But first drink a cup of wine with me so that I can wish you luck."

The leader drained the cup, jumped on his horse, and disappeared with his troop in another direction.

But the merchant had now something to think about while the caravan was setting off on its long journey into the desert.

"I wonder who the child is," he thought. "Ah well, Herod won't get him now. Nor his ring — I'll get that yet."

Through the desert

The caravan threaded its way through the desert. First came the leading camel with the head driver, then the merchant on the oldest camel, followed by all the others in a long line. Last of all trotted the little donkey with Mary and the baby, and Joseph beside them.

"Just wait," mumbled the merchant, "soon the donkey will collapse in the sand. Then they'll be glad of my help."

So he told the camel-driver at the end of the line not to lose sight of the donkey.

But the proud camels slowed their pace so that the donkey could keep up.

The drivers yelled and urged the camels on, but it did not make any difference, the camels just would not go any faster.

"I think the beasts have been bewitched," said the head driver. "What's the matter with them?"

"Make them go faster!" said the merchant. "You promised a quick journey."

But really he was quite glad that the little family did not trail too far behind.

Even so the donkey could not help growing tired. When it was time to set up camp towards evening he had already dropped a good way behind, though he tried bravely to keep up with the others.

"Poor little donkey," said the leading camel, when he had caught up at last, "are you very tired? We

109

tried to keep to your pace so that you could keep up with us."

"Oh," said the donkey, "I'll get over it, as long as I can get a rest. But I think we are going such a terribly long way from home, and I do so long for Nazareth. All my friends are waiting there for us. They must be almost crazy with longing to see the child."

"Little donkey," said the oldest camel, "Egypt is still a long way away. For many days you will travel with your tail towards Nazareth."

"Oh," said the donkey sadly, "but the angel has told us to go, and I see we must, because of the wicked king."

The next day the desert was even hotter.

"Oh, it feels as if the sun is lying here on the earth and is burning up every living thing!" sighed the donkey.

Occasionally he got a mouthful of precious water which the merchant sold to Joseph from his huge leather bottle.

During the afternoon the heat was even worse. Suddenly the donkey saw the angel beckoning him to turn off to the left. The donkey obeyed at once, but gave out a piercing cry to warn the camels that danger was approaching.

"What's the matter?" cried Joseph.

"Better let him do what he wants," said Mary, "He always knows which is the right way. I believe he's seen the angel again."

"What's the matter, little donkey?" cried the leading camel.

"The angel told me to go this way," answered the donkey.

The camel turned round and cantered back to the donkey. All the others followed. The camel-drivers yelled and screamed. The merchant woke from his dozing.

110

"What on earth's gone wrong?" he grumbled.

"The camels have all gone mad," answered the head driver. "The donkey brayed and they all turned round in spite of their drivers. I have never known them to do that before."

"Turn the camels round again," commanded the merchant.

"They won't," came the answer.

The men were completely helpless and had to go where the big animals took them.

The angel had led the donkey to a hollow in the ground protected by huge blocks of stone. There he told the donkey to stop, and in the next minute all the camels had come up.

"The angel wants us to stay here," declared the donkey.

"Are you sure you've seen right?" said the leading camel mildly. "You must be very tired and it's quite common to see mirages in the desert — to see oases and such like."

"No," said the donkey, "I really did see the angel."

"What's gone wrong with you?" barked the merchant at Joseph. "Why did you lead the donkey here?"

"I didn't," said Joseph. "He went by himself; he's sure to have seen again the good angel that God has sent to help us on our way to Egypt."

"I think you've all gone quite crazy," snapped the merchant. "You and your donkey and the camels and the drivers that let them do what they want."

Suddenly he gave a shout and pointed ahead. Far away a black cloud could be seen.

"A sandstorm!" he cried. "The Lord be praised for leading us to this hollow where we may find shelter."

Camp was got ready at full speed. Hardly had they finished before a frightful storm broke upon them. The sand whipped by and all was dark.

"If we had carried on out there our lives would have been in danger," said the merchant. "This storm is the worst I have ever met, but we're all right in here. How lucky we got here!"

"It was the angel of the Lord who led the donkey here," said Mary.

"Yes it must have been," agreed the headman, "but I don't understand it all the same."

"It's quite understandable really," said Joseph. "God sent his angel to help us. We cannot see the angel, but our little donkey can. That's why we can safely follow him wherever he goes."

"Yes," said the leader, "I've never felt so safe in a storm as I do now with you."

"Nor have we," said the other camel-drivers. "Now we understand why you won't sell your donkey."

"And I won't try any more to make you to sell him either," said the merchant.

After that they all sat silent, listening to the roar of the storm. The only thing that could sometimes be heard above its noise was the happy chortling of the little baby.

By the morning of the next day it was quiet again.

"I have a suggestion to make to you," said the merchant, who did not want to lose sight of Joseph and the ring. "You and your wife can ride on camels and that will make it easier for the donkey to keep up."

Joseph and Mary spoke together and then Joseph said: "We like your idea, and we thank you heartily for wanting to spare our little donkey."

The camels began to get excited. Which one of them was to carry the child on his back? Then they moved up carefully trying to look very quiet and very pious.

One of the pack-camels was chosen, and his load was shared out among the others. Mary now sat on the strong animal who went striding along majestically through the desert.

"Look," said the driver, "the camel really knows he's carrying something special."

But the donkey trotted gloomily behind. He felt so forlorn not having Mary on his back.

"Here am I, going along, and I'm now only an ordinary donkey," he thought. "No longer Mary's special donkey. It's much heavier going without her weight. I wish I could lay my head on Joseph's shoulder now and again for a bit of comforting. And I can't hear the baby. I can't bear it."

113

But the pack-camel was very proud that evening and never stopped telling the others what the woman had said and how the child had patted him as his mother held his little hand.

The next morning it was found that the camel had hurt his foot a little and was limping a bit. They put his loads back on him and another animal was chosen for Mary to ride on. And this sort of thing happened every morning. Each new camel managed to carry the child and his mother for one day only, and then by morning something had gone wrong with him. The animals thought this a very fair arrangement, but the drivers were very puzzled.

"It seems as if that's how the camels want it," said the head man who really understood his animals well.

But the donkey grew more and more wretched. It had been a long time since he had done anything for Mary. All he had to do now was to trot behind the others. He hung his head and looked miserable.

"You're not standing up well to the heat," Joseph would say at the end of the day, "even though you're not carrying anything."

But the donkey only turned his head away and would not let Joseph stroke him. Yet when Mary came he could not help himself, he just had to rub his nose against her cheek.

"We'll soon be in Egypt," she comforted him. "Then it will be just you and me and the baby again."

One day there was no more water left.

"We've been held up by the sandstorm," said the head man, "but with luck we'll reach a well before evening. There's a little oasis a half day's journey from here."

That was the worst day of the whole journey. Everyone was plagued with thirst. The donkey walked as if in a dream and his feet felt as heavy as lead. He was wet with sweat and completely covered with dust.

"What does it matter now if I die in the desert?" he thought. "Joseph and Mary can manage just as well without me. I am only a hindrance."

And the donkey collapsed and lay in the hot sand.

"We haven't time to wait for him," said the headman. "We've got to get to the well before we all perish."

Joseph asked if he could get off his camel.

"I'll manage to reach the well with the donkey," he said. "I can't let him die here."

He went back to the donkey and talked to him and comforted him. At last he succeeded in getting him on his feet; but they were both tired out and thirsty as they staggered forward.

"Hold out!" said Joseph. "The oasis is over there and you'll be able to drink as much as you can."

But there was no water there. The storm had choked up the well and buried the water deep in sand.

The men were tired out and bad-tempered.

"It's all your fault," said the merchant to Joseph, "yours and your donkey's. It's him who's kept us back. Otherwise we should have reached Egypt by now."

"The Lord will help us," said Mary gently and went over to the donkey. She was carrying the baby in her arms.

"I wouldn't mind if he did," grumbled the merchant. "But I can't see it happening."

But Mary bent over the donkey that was lying half dead at her feet. Suddenly the child began to laugh. It sounded like a babbling brook.

"Listen to the child," said the headman, "only a very little child could laugh now."

"Shut him up!" said the merchant who had fever and was suffering badly from thirst. "Oh, is there no one who can sell me a mug of water for a gold coin," he moaned.

No one answered.

"O little child," whispered Mary, "stroke our donkey. He'll feel better if you just touch him," and she took the child's hand and guided it to the donkey's head. The baby chortled as if he would say something. He wriggled with eagerness. The tired animal opened his listless eyes and looked at the little one. What could that be that he was trying to say? The donkey tried to read the answer in the child's clear eyes.

Good gracious! What was that? The Angel! Beckoning! The donkey stirred and lifted his head, and really and truly the angel stood there, beckoning. The donkey heaved himself up and tottered towards him.

"The donkey has seen the angel," whispered Mary. "Heaven be praised, now we shall have some water."

"Water!" cried everyone and followed the donkey in a long straggling line. The angel led the donkey a few hundred yards out into the desert to where there was a clear well.

Joseph brought the water to Mary.

"No, give it to the merchant first," she said, "he's fainted."

When Joseph brought the fresh water to the man's lips he came to his senses.

"What kind of water is that?" he asked, "It has made me quite fresh right away."

After that all the men sat talking far into the night about the miracle that had happened and how they had been rescued thanks to Mary's little donkey.

In Egypt

A green plain now spread out before the happy gaze of Joseph and Mary. Far off they could see a broad gleaming streak. The camel-drivers said that it was the Nile, Egypt's famous river.

"Very soon now the ring will be mine," thought the merchant gleefully, "what a beautiful ring it is. I could hardly restrain myself when I saw the baby playing with it. What a toy for a baby!"

But a faint voice whispered in the merchant's heart: "Do you really think it is right to take the ring in payment for the little that you have done? Isn't it rather they who have helped you? How was it with the sandstorm and the well?" But the merchant silenced that voice.

"I'll do more for them," he thought, "Supposing I see to it that Joseph gets some work in Egypt and the family a house to live in, then I've more than earned the ring. Joseph can't really find work here by himself. All the same it will be sad to part from them," he sighed. "It's funny how I've got to like them: quiet old Joseph and Mary who's always gentle and happy. And the baby, I wish he were my boy! I've never liked anyone as much as him, and fancy, I'm even fond of their little donkey. Yes, there's something about them. . . . Sometimes I wonder who they really are. But I'll get them a roof over their heads anyway."

They came to quite a big village. There the merchant had a friend whom he was in the habit of visiting. He spoke to him about Joseph.

"Listen," he said to Joseph afterwards. "A friend of mine has a garden here in the village where he grows balsam. It has got a bit wild recently, but he'll take you on to look after it. There's a little house you can put in order and live in."

Joseph and Mary of course were delighted.

"Are you an angel in disguise?" cried Mary. "Sometimes I have almost thought that!"

The merchant blushed.

"How can we repay you for your goodness," said Joseph, "what could we give you?"

The merchant swallowed hard and said: "The ring!"

Joseph and Mary looked at each other.

"It belongs to the child," said Joseph, "I don't know if we can give it to you."

The baby was sitting in Mary's lap, playing with the ring. It was as if he understood for he held it out to the merchant with a happy little chirp.

"See, he's giving it to you," said Mary. "Take it. But you should also hear what kind of a ring it is, because it is no ordinary gold finger-ring. The child received it from a very wise and wealthy man, who said: 'This is the ring of truth, and if anyone wears the ring who is upright and true the pearl will shine beautifully, but if the wearer has mischief in his mind and tries to deceive or cheat anyone, the pearl will lose its sheen and beauty.' But you are a good man and you can wear the ring."

The merchant stood there with the ring in his hand — but poor fellow! Now he possessed the valuable piece and did not dare to put it on; no, he did not even dare to look at it!

Then the headman called. The caravan was ready to move on and the merchant had to go. Hastily he took leave of Joseph and Mary, kissed the child and hurried away, holding the ring hard in his clenched hand. Turning round he called: "I'll come back. I promise to help you on your journey home to your own country again when the time comes."

"The Lord be with you," Mary called back.

Joseph and Mary lived in the Egyptian village for many years. Everybody there thought that they were ordinary people. The women often came to their house to have a chat with Mary. They would admire her boy and were never tired of praising him. He was so gentle and strong and kind.

"You never saw such a child in all the land of the Jews," one woman would say. "He's like an angel from heaven. But Mary, could you lend me a little flour, mine's all finished and my little girl is hungry, she's not nearly so strong and healthy as your boy."

Then Mary would take out her small store and give it to her neighbour.

"Your child looks like a king's son," another would say, "Something great will come of that child, Mary. But could you lend me some oil, for my cruse is quite empty?"

And Mary would take out her jar of oil and give it to her neighbour who would go back to her own home happily with it.

Even by now nobody in the village really knew who the child was. But the animals had found out within a few hours of their arrival. First of all it was the dog. He had been sniffing around in the garden and heard the baby chortling. Mary had laid him in the warm sand under a rustling palm-tree. The dog was curious and drew near. As soon as he saw that the child was left on his own he came up and began to nuzzle him.

"Don't hurt him," called the donkey who was tethered to a tree.

The baby stretched out his little chubby hand and stuck it right into the dog's mouth. The donkey hardly dared to breathe.

"Mind out," he whispered to the child, "Mind out."

But the dog licked the hand very carefully and then began to roll around on the ground and play till the little one was laughing happily.

"What child is that?" the dog asked the surprised donkey. "There's something special about him. He's not like other children. It's so lovely to be near him, I have never felt anything like it before. Is he an angel and no human child?"

"He is the one who is to be the Good Shepherd," the donkey told him.

"What are you saying?" cried the dog, "and I went and licked his face!"

Just then the neighbour's cat came along waving her tail ready to jump up on to the roof. It was such fun sitting up there and driving all the dogs mad.

"Come here, cat," shouted the dog eagerly, "come and listen."

The cat was so surprised that she stood still.

"What are you up to now?" she hissed. "Do you think you can trick me?"

"Oh no," said the dog, "but come and see the new baby. Who do you think he is? Guess!"

The baby stretched out his arms to the cat who shot forward to him and began to purr and put her front paws gently on him.

"Mind the child," warned the dog, "Don't you see who it is?"

"He looks just like an ordinary child," thought the cat, "but it does feel good when he touches me — the way I was licked when I was little."

"Who is he then?" she asked aloud.

"The Good Shepherd," said the dog.

"The one that the whole world's been waiting for from the beginning?" asked the cat.

"Yes," said the donkey, "that's him."

Some birds came swooping over the cat's head.

120

They had caught sight of her and thought that they would tease her.

"Stop that!" called the cat to the birds. "Don't disturb the baby. Can't you see he's just gone to sleep?"

"What baby is that?" the curious birds wanted to know as they swooped down close past the cat again.

"Hey, be careful," said the cat, "you'll wake him."

The birds perched in the tree and looked at the child.

"Come and have a good look at him," said the cat.

"Ha, trust you," mocked the birds, "oh no, we know what you're like!"

"I won't touch you. I promise," said the cat.

One or two birds risked coming down on to the ground but well out of reach of the cat.

"Oh what a lovely baby! Look how he smiles in his sleep," they twittered.

"Do you know what child that is?" asked the dog.

"No," said one of the birds, "he looks like an angel."

"Do you know what angels look like?" asked the cat.

"*Yes I do*! I was in the Land of Judah in winter and it was quite full of angels. They were singing because of a child who had come from heaven to a town called Bethlehem."

"I saw them too," said a second bird.

"We were talking to some birds who had come with his mother," chattered a third.

"You should have heard how the angels sang," chirped another. "We could never learn to sing like that, but we did learn a cradle song from those birds and it went like this."

The birds were now all singing so happily and at the same time so peacefully that Mary came out and said: "Those can't be my birds from Nazareth, can they?"

Smiling she scattered a handful of corn for them. When they came to eat it she saw that they were not her birds after all.

"That's funny," she said, "you sing just like my little songsters at home."

"But that *is* the child's mother," chirped the birds, "and so that *is* the child that the angels sang for."

"That's right," said the dog, "and he is to become the Good Shepherd."

"But how did they get here?" asked the birds. "right to the banks of the Nile."

"I shall tell you," said the donkey.

But the little donkey had hardly begun before one of the birds cried:

"But it *was you* who were with them. You're their little donkey!"

"Yes, yes," piped the other birds, "it's the same little donkey."

And then they listened ever so quietly to all that the donkey had to tell about the flight into Egypt. When he had finished the birds said: "We are so glad that the Good Shepherd has come here to our country."

"But we're not going to stay here always," said the donkey.

"Then why did you come here?" the birds wanted to know.

The donkey told them about the wicked king.

"We must work together and see to it that no harm comes to the child," said the cat earnestly. "You birds must be our scouts. As soon as you hear of anything that is not good, come here and tell us. The dog and I will take turns to keep watch when the donkey is away at work. Because Egypt is also a dangerous country, and you never know. . . ."

"Yes, that sounds good," thought the dog and the

birds. They wanted to see that nothing should happen to the child.

"Is that really necessary?" asked the donkey. "It's so peaceful here."

"Don't you be too sure!" said the dog.

"The angels will help us," said the donkey.

But the days went by very smoothly without any disturbance or excitement other than when a caravan arrived. Then there would be hustle and bustle and shouting for an hour or two, and soon the village would settle down sleepily and quietly again.

One day, however, things nearly went wrong.

King Herod who was angry because he had not got hold of the boy sent a message to Egypt asking the Egyptians to let his soldiers cross the border to look for the child as he thought that the child might possibly have got into their country.

And that is how the soldiers come to the village.

Mary was just clearing out an old tumbledown cottage standing among some rotting tree-trunks. It had not been used for many years, and now Mary wanted to clear away the rubbish and sweep the cottage clean so that Joseph could keep his tools there. The boy had grown much bigger now and could crawl about. He was playing now with the cat outside, while Joseph and the donkey worked in an outlying corner of the huge gardens.

The soldiers rode up to the village. They went into the houses asking about the family fleeing from the Land of Judah. But they could not find out anything because no one would tell them anything about Joseph and Mary. They searched every house in the village but could not find a trace of them.

The swallows nesting above the door of the first house saw the soldiers but did not know that that meant danger.

123

But a shining angel appeared before them, pointed to Mary's garden and whispered: "Hasten and hide the child!"

Off flew the birds at once and then they piped together: "Soldiers! They're looking for the child!"

"Where shall we hide him?" wailed the cat all of a fright.

"Into the hut!" said the dog rushing up.

The birds flew down on to the ground and chirped noisily in front of the boy. He understood right away what they meant, because he crawled quickly into the dark hut. Mary however, thought he would be in the way and wanted to carry him out again, but the birds all fluttered round her head and cheeped so woefully that she understood that they wanted something special. She went out and listened. Then she heard the trampling of hooves. Horses! That meant soldiers.

Mary clutched the baby to her breast and drew back into the hut as far as she could. Oh, why had she swept and cleaned up just today? Now the hut looked so clean that the soldiers would certainly search here. She wanted to run out and look for another hiding place.

But the birds were still very troubled. They fluttered and cheeped and sent Mary back in again. Then some swallows came with spiders in their beaks. They put them on the old trees by the hut and immediately the spiders began to make a huge web which hung down in front of the doorway. The dog pawed some dust on to the swept floor so that it soon looked as dirty as before. And when the soldiers came to the garden the cat was lying in front of the doorway of the hut yawning.

The soldiers looked into Mary's little cottage, but there was no one at home. They took no notice of Joseph and the donkey. They cast a glance at the little hut, but one of them said: "No one has set foot inside there for years."

"We'd better have a look all the same," said another.

"You go then," said the first, "if you want a spider's web round your helmet!"

They all laughed and rode away, and soon the thunder of their hooves showed that they were leaving the village.

"Joseph," called Mary.

Joseph came hurrying.

"Soldiers!" said Mary. "They were looking for us."

"Oh," said Joseph, alarmed. "Heaven be praised that they didn't find us!"

"The birds got the boy into the hut and made me stay quiet in there. The dog kicked up earth all over the floor and the spiders filled the doorway with cobwebs almost before I could wink!"

"Ah," said Joseph, "We ought never to fear, for the good angels protect us and they get the animals to help them."

"But how can the animals know who our child is, Joseph?"

Joseph only shook his head and smiled at Mary who was scattering corn for the birds and putting milk into a bowl for the cat and the dog.

The little donkey smiled to himself.

"Many thanks to you all, good friends," he said later to the dog and the cat and the birds. "You did that very well."

"Yes," said the cat, "didn't we say that we should watch over the child?"

"And you didn't think it would be necessary, did you?" said the dog, "Well, now you see."

"Hm," said the little donkey. "But I said that the angels would help us."

Meantime the baby had got his hands full of cobwebs and a big spider was crawling right over his forefinger. He was sitting quite still just looking at it.

Good news

From time to time the rich merchant came by. Whenever he passed through the little village he always took time to go out to the balsam garden and visit Joseph and Mary. Sometimes he brought with him a fine piece of wood for Joseph to make something of. Sometimes he brought some beautiful material for Mary, and he always brought a gift for the boy.

When he came the first time the boy had just learnt to walk.

"Fancy him walking already," cried the merchant surprised. "And how well he manages. See how he can keep his balance."

To hear the merchant you would think that it was a marvel that the boy could toddle at all.

But Joseph smiled and said, "All little children learn to walk as long as they've got healthy legs."

Next time the merchant came to visit, the child could talk and say "father" and "mother" and a few other simple words.

Oh such a clever child! The merchant had never heard the like before, so clearly and properly did he say each word. Surely he would be a great orator in Israel one day.

But Mary laughed and said that the boy was no better at talking than other children of his age.

But now the merchant had not been seen for a long time. Joseph and Mary sometimes talked about him and wondered if he had given up travelling to Egypt.

More often they wondered whether the time would soon come for them to go back home.

But no one longed for the journey home more than the donkey. Of course it was nice playing with the boy who was growing up so fast and learning to walk and talk. But it would have been nicer still to have been able to share that joy with all his friends back in Nazareth. How they must be waiting! The little frisky kids and lambs! Oh they must have grown up long since, but the donkey was sure that they still were yearning just as much for Mary and the child! And he could never forget that he had promised to bring them home again. "Sometimes I think I'm beginning to grow old," he thought. "My legs are getting a bit stiff and it's going to be hard for me to cross the great desert again. I hope it won't be too long now. And my eyes are getting dimmer than they used to be. Supposing I shouldn't be able to see the angel. How should we get along then?"

"Mary," said Joseph one day, "I think our little donkey's beginning to get old. He can't do as much as he used to, and I wonder how his eyes are doing."

Mary lifted up the donkey's head and looked into his eyes.

"They are just as beautiful as before," she said, "and he looks at me so lovingly that my heart overflows with gratitude."

"But he stumbled over a tree trunk today and yesterday he bumped into a tree. He can't see properly where he's going any more."

"My dear," said Mary, "then we must be doubly careful with him."

Joseph and Mary stroked the donkey more often than before and fed him the best things they could scrape together, and Joseph often carried the burdens himself even if he had to go back and forth several times.

In this way the donkey found plenty of time to play with the child. Joseph had made a saddle for him and he soon learned to ride even though he was so little. Then the donkey did not feel at all that his legs were stiff and his eyes dim, but would set off at a gallop while the little boy cheered and halloed and rose high in the saddle so that all the other children in the village came running along to watch. And then they each would get a little turn at riding.

In between times the donkey would lie down and rest and the boy would sit beside him and talk and talk.

"How well the two understand each other," observed Mary.

One fine morning Joseph said, "Mary, be glad. We're going home!"

"Oh, are we really, Joseph? How wonderful! How do you know?"

"The angel spoke to me in a dream and said, 'The wicked king is dead. Take Mary and the boy with you and go home to your own country?' "

Mary clapped her hands and her face shone. "Thanks be to God! Home at last!"

And she lifted up the boy and said:

"My child, now at last you will see your home."

"Home?" wondered the boy.

But Joseph looked searchingly at the little donkey. Would the donkey be up to it?

That same evening the quiet village was roused by a merry jingling sound.

"There's a caravan coming," said Mary. "I hear the camels' bells. I wonder if it isn't our good friend, the merchant, who's coming."

"Yes he did promise to help us on our way home, and I'm sure God has sent him now at this moment," said Joseph.

And it was the merchant right enough.

He was greatly pleased to see how big the boy had grown.

"Oh, what a fine child!" he cried. "A royal child! And now you can return home as the wicked King Herod is dead. Be ready early tomorrow morning and we'll start on our journey through the desert."

The journey home

"Well, well!" said the camels, "If it isn't Mary's little donkey! Are you going home now? That's nice!"

"Oh," said two new camels after introducing themselves with their very best manners, "are you Mary's little donkey? We've been told you're the cleverest donkey in the world, and that you can see angels. Is that true?"

"I used to be able," said the donkey, "but I must confess my eyes have grown rather dim lately, so I'm not quite sure if I can now."

"I'm sure you'll be able to if necessary," said the oldest camel kindly.

So the long journey home began. The boy gave a happy shout when he was allowed to ride a camel, but as soon as the company halted he was with the little donkey holding him by the neck and whispering his secrets into the donkey's ear.

"I'm no good any more," thought the donkey sadly. "I'm only a burden."

It was as if the boy understood, for he said his donkey was the best playmate and friend in all the world, and how a little boy should get along without a donkey was more than he could understand. Then the donkey forgot his awful tiredness and his feet stopped aching. He rubbed his nose caressingly against the boy's cheek.

"He has healing in his hands," the donkey told the camels.

They thought so too, for when one of them got a bad bite from a horse-fly, he was made better again when the boy laid his cool hand on the burning swelling.

This time the journey went well. No sandstorm came sweeping along to force the travellers to seek shelter, and when they came to the infrequent wells they found them full of water.

But they soon became aware that the nights were not so peaceful. Lots of wild animals roamed around the caravan when it was time to set up camp, and as soon as night came on the travellers sensed a terrible prowling going on round them in the darkness. Jackals howled eerily so that the blood froze in the men's veins, and the roar of the lions rolled like thunder over the desert. The travellers kept their fires burning all night, and the camel-drivers took turns at keeping watch.

One night it was worse than ever. There was a roaring and howling and barking the like of which no one had ever heard before, and only the boy could sleep through it. The camels and the donkey trembled. The men were anxious and uneasy. At last however everyone fell asleep and towards morning even the watchmen dozed off.

The moon stood high in the vault of the sky, shining so brightly that it was almost like day. The desert sands gleamed like silver. The little donkey woke up because it was suddenly so silent all around.

He stood for a moment blinking in the soft moonlight, and his dim eyes looked out over the desert. He thought how very beautiful it was.

"That's good," he thought. "The wild animals have gone away. They've realized at last that it's no use coming too near for the fire is burning all night. It's good to have a fire, it protects us and scares them away. Well, I think I can sleep for a bit longer. It's not morning yet. How soundly Mary is sleeping, and Joseph, and the little. . ."

The donkey blinked, then he looked again, but no, he could not see the boy. He got very worried and he started to go round the camp searching. Not a trace of the child anywhere.

"Where is he?" wondered the donkey. "Where? A lion couldn't have . . . no impossible! But where is he? . . . Perhaps after all a lion. . . "

The donkey searched through the camp once more. No sign of the boy. The poor donkey wandered out alone into the desert. He had to find out what had happened to the child.

"Have the wild animals killed him? If they have, they might as well kill me too. What is there left for me to live for?" he thought miserably.

Some way off some big bright stones stood out sharply against the sky. The donkey went towards them, but when he got nearer he smelled the smell of lions. He stopped abruptly for it seemed a bit grizzly just to walk straight into the wild beasts' mouths. Oh, his whole body was trembling. Then he heard a happy little laugh. The boy!

Oh well, he'd have to go on now, come what may. The donkey went forward and called to his little friend. Soon he saw that the stones were alive. They were huge lions lying in a circle round the child who was sitting on the ground. One of the lions knocked him over playfully but carefully with his mighty paw. The boy rolled over. He certainly thought it was a good game because he was soon on his feet calling, "Again", and once more the lion boxed him over. Then he went up to the lion and playfully blew into his eyes. The donkey hardly dared to breathe, but the lion did not mind. Then the boy tickled the lion's big nose and the lion curled up and purred like a giant cat.

Another lion nudged the boy gently in the ribs asking to be stroked, while the jackals lay around wagging their tails, and one of them pushed his way in among the lions and licked the boy's foot.

Then the boy noticed the little donkey and called out happily. The lions turned round and looked at the donkey, who felt himself trembling worse than before.

"Don't be afraid," said one of the lions. "We won't do you any harm tonight. But why won't humans let us greet the Good Shepherd?"

"How did you know it was him?" asked the donkey astonished.

"The birds in Egypt have spread the tidings far and wide, and we have followed after him all this time to see him and greet him, but the humans would not let us."

"They did not understand that's what you wanted," said the donkey.

"But tonight he came out himself to us. We all had given one great yell together and he woke up and came out to us and he wasn't afraid, no, not a bit."

"Oh no, he's not afraid of anything," said the donkey. "But what do you want with him? Wild animals don't need a shepherd, do they?"

"Don't you know," answered the lion, "that it has been said: 'The day shall come when all animals shall be friends and live in peace with one another. Panthers and lions shall live together with cows and asses and lambs, and a little child shall lead them.' And who else should that child be but this little one here? The Good Shepherd!" And the great animal laid his head humbly against the child's leg.

"But how do you know all this?" asked the donkey in wonder.

"God has ordained it from the beginning of time. The wind speaks of it and the water sings of it. One must only take the time to listen to it. Isn't that true, little one?"

The boy nodded earnestly.

134

"Just imagine, we knew straight away it was him," said another lion, "for when he came we felt so safe and peaceful, and none could harm another."

Now a third lion came up.

"Would you like a ride?" he asked, and lay down. The boy understood, for he tried to climb up on to the back of the powerful animal. Finally he succeeded and he sat there proudly holding on to the lion's mane. Then the ride began; and you never saw anything like it! The lion bounded along and the boy whooped with delight.

Meanwhile away over in the camp Joseph had woken up. Immediately he woke the other men and they armed themselves with sticks and burning firebrands and went in search of the child, fearing the worst.

But who should come to meet them but the boy riding on a lion! Ten paces away from the astonished men the lion halted, lay down on the ground and let the child slide off his back. Then the lion turned round and disappeared as quickly as he had come.

Joseph took the boy in his arms. "Where have you been, dear boy?"

"With the wild animals."

"Buy why? didn't you know it was dangerous?"

"They called me and so I went."

"O my boy, we were all so afraid," said Joseph.

"But it wasn't dangerous at all," said the boy. "The animals were all so nice."

"What manner of child is that?" wondered the camel-drivers. "He was riding on a lion as proudly as a king on his horse. Are we dreaming or are we awake?"

The next night the boy woke up when the animals called him. Joseph noticed that he had got up and told him to lie down again; but the boy answered that the animals were longing very much to see him. He just had to go then.

"Go then, my dear," said Mary. "You will be as safe among the animals of the wild as among the dogs and cats of Egypt. No animal can hurt you."

For three nights the boy played with the animals in the desert. He had the same fun each time and more and more animals came along. On the last night the lions took him with them to a little oasis miles away. There little monkeys picked the most gorgeous fruit for him.

In the morning no one in the camp would believe his story, but when he brought out a bunch of dates they were all amazed, and the headman said: "We used to marvel greatly at Mary's little donkey that could see angels, but we must marvel even more at this child. Is he an angel that has come down to earth? Who else could be as safe amongst the wild beasts as on his mother's knee?"

Certainly the days were terribly hot in the desert and the way was not one bit shorter than before, but the boy was so radiantly happy and cheerful at all times that both the people and the animals forgot their tiredness and thirst. And it was quite impossible to be unfriendly or in a bad mood when he was about.

"Well, well, look!" said the camels one day. "Have we got through the desert already? Over there are the mountains of Judah."

"How quickly this journey has passed," said the camel-drivers. "We'll soon be there."

When they came to the place where the road branched off to Jerusalem Joseph and Mary had to part from their fellow-travellers.

"Many, many thanks for all your help," said Joseph to the merchant.

"I have been more than rewarded," replied he.

"Was the ring so valuable?" asked Joseph wonderingly.

"The ring! Certainly it is very, very valuable, and I haven't yet dared to put it on. Soon perhaps I shall do so. But I meant that it has been a great joy to help you and Mary and the boy, and to be your friend is reward enough."

"You are so good," said Mary. "We shall never forget you. If your way takes you to Nazareth any time, do come and visit us."

"I have never travelled through that town, but for you I will go there. I must see how the boy is growing. Upon my word, one day he will be great."

"Farewell, little donkey," said the camels. "Perhaps we shall never meet again, but we'll never forget you and Joseph and Mary and the child. No one has ever been so good to us as they, and when the boy is present the camel-drivers are much more friendly than otherwise. They don't drive us so hard and they give us more to eat."

"Farewell," said the little donkey. "I shall never forget all your help."

Joseph and Mary stood and watched the caravan drawing away as it headed for Jerusalem. They themselves had before them a few days' journey to the north. But it was along well-known roads they were to go, and it was their own countrymen that they would be meeting. They were back in their home country. It was early spring and it smelled of thousands of flowers. The donkey snatched at some green blades.

"I'd forgotten how good the grass tastes here at home," he thought.

"My dear little donkey," said Mary, "now you must carry all our baggage home. Will you manage that?"

The donkey twitched his long tail happily.

"Look Joseph, how lively he is! He knows we'll soon be home."

"But it is a big load," said Joseph. "The merchant has given us so many parting gifts."

"I can walk the whole way," said Mary. "I feel so fresh now that I can breathe the air of our own country again. The boy can walk too for he's so big and strong now. See how lightly he runs about. And if need be I can carry him sometimes."

"Yes, that way we'll manage fine," said Joseph. "And I can take some of the baggage on my back."

So they travelled towards Nazareth, Joseph with a big bundle on his back, the little donkey loaded with as much as he could carry and Mary with the little boy. He danced on ahead of them so lightly that it seemed he had invisible wings.

The long waiting

"We've been away such a long time now," said Joseph. "I don't think anyone will remember us any more.

"Oh yes, they will," said Mary. "My sister will be thinking of us, you can be sure. And all our friends. And the animals at home."

Yes there were many who remembered them and missed them.

First there was the old man who owned the tumble-down stable in Bethlehem.

"I wonder what's become of them," he would say when he met the shepherds. "I can't get them out of my thoughts. They fled from wicked Herod, but how could they survive in the desert? I'm sure his soldiers caught up with them and killed them."

"The desert is also very dangerous for lone travellers," said the shepherds. "We must really fear the worst."

"How can you talk like that?" said the youngest shepherd, who was called Reuben. "Could God have let them perish when he himself sent the child to earth? No, I believe they are all right somewhere far away. And now that King Herod's dead they'll come back, you'll see. I'd just love to see the child again. Do you remember that night?"

"Yes; do you remember the shining ring round the child's head?" said Reuben's grandfather, "Almost like a crown, and it was only starlight shining on him"

"I shall never forget the angels' song," said Reuben's father.

"I wish they'd come soon," sighed the old man in the stable. "I feel I haven't much longer to live. My heart tells me that."

"They'll come soon," said Reuben, "and I'm longing to see their little donkey too. I did like him so much."

In a little town not so very far from Bethlehem there lived three men who also often talked about Joseph and Mary. They were honest men and who had been robbers at one time.

"Wasn't it a grand feeling the morning we left the robbers' den," the young one would say. "Wasn't it fine to work and not just go and hatch out wicked plans."

"Yes, and how I enjoyed the birds singing that first time," the second went on.

"But since then," mused the oldest, "we have often found it hard to earn a living and we've been hungry sometimes."

"More than once I've been tempted to go out and steal," said the youngest.

"I don't think I can keep off it much longer," said the second. "When I get hungry I feel my fingers itching."

"It would be marvellous if good Mary were to come here," exclaimed the oldest. "If only I could see her and talk with her I should be able to put up with poverty again."

"Me too," said the friend of the birds.

"And me," added the youngest. "But I don't think we'll see her again."

"I wonder what became of them," wondered the oldest.

And there were the children in the poor house where Joseph and Mary and the donkey had stayed on the first night of their journey to Bethlehem.

"They never seem to be coming back," said the older girl, "and Mary promised so faithfully to let me hold her little baby."

"And I was to look after the nice donkey," said the boy who had cried at that time because his father had not got a donkey. "And I've got so much hay for the donkey now, it'll last a whole year!"

He had been gathering hay all this time and he had a big, big stack.

"Remember how nice it was," said his big sister, "when they let us go with them some of the way."

"And they let us ride," said the others, "it was the best treat we ever had."

"I do long to see Mary," sighed the older sister. "No one is so good and gentle as she."

"I want to play with her baby," said the little one who had now grown into quite a big girl.

But of course the ones who missed them most were those at home in Nazareth.

"Why doesn't Mary come?" sighed her sister. "I wonder where she is."

"They'll never come home again," said her husband. The sister was deeply troubled.

"I can't manage her animals much longer," she complained. "It takes too much time to look after them and get fodder for them as well, especially when I've got my own to care for too. It was all right as long as old Judith was able to help, but now she can't walk at all and I have to lend her a hand instead."

"We'll have to sell the animals," said her husband, "and we better sell the house and the bit of land too."

"No, no!" cried the wife, "we can't do that. At least not yet! Supposing they came back soon!"

"The rich potter said yesterday that he would like to buy the lot. He'll give us a good price."

"Not yet. We'll wait a bit," his wife begged. "I'll manage a bit longer."

"The potter wants to buy right away," said the man.

"But he's not a nice man," sighed the sister. "Mary's animals will have a rough time with him, and they're not used to anything but kindness. No, let me try a little while yet."

But who could miss them more than the animals on Mary's homestead.

"Where has the little donkey got to?" the little lambs and kids had wailed while they were growing up. One fine day they were no longer lambs and kids but fully grown sheep and goats, but they still missed them just as much. They told their own lambs and kids how Mary would be coming home soon, and that she would have her little child with her. And she would be riding on the ablest cleverest donkey in all the world.

"Will they come soon, mother?" bleated the new little lambs.

And the new little kids sprang about and kept on asking: "Do you think they'll come tomorrow, mother?"

"Don't pester so much," said the old nanny-goat, "Or they won't come at all."

It was the same with the birds of Nazareth. They had indeed flown home with the news of the birth of the child and there had been great rejoicing among the animals of Nazareth. They had all believed that Joseph and Mary would be coming home with their child in just a few days. But Mary and Joseph had not yet appeared. Where had they got to?

The birds waited and waited, but they did not forget. Again and again new little birds sat in their nests and piped: "Won't they come soon, mother?"

142

Happy travellers

And now the donkey was on his way home with Joseph and Mary and the child, although hardly anyone knew.

As they were coming near to Bethlehem Mary said, "We must go and visit the old man. He was so good to us."

Then the donkey tripped along so lightly on the road he knew of old. No angel was needed to show him which way to go.

How happy the old man was to see them. He talked and talked.

"There you've come at last!" he said. "Indeed I should have known that something was going to happen, because last night I dreamed I was walking in the gardens of paradise, and that could only mean that God intends to take me there now for my heart cannot cope with earthly life any more. But I did not want to die before I had seen you and the child again. And how big and fine the boy has grown. He looks just like the angels I saw in my dream last night. And tomorrow you must look up the shepherds when you go by."

"Oh my dear!" said Mary surprised. "Haven't they forgotten us?"

"Forgotten you!" said the old man. "I just wonder who could ever forget you!"

And so they came to sleep the night in the stable again. But of course the boy was much too big to find room in the crib. He lay on the straw between the black cow and the sheep.

"Fancy seeing him again," they whispered contentedly to each other.

Reuben had taken his sheep to the pasture land to graze. He was almost fully grown now, a powerful lad with broad shoulders and an open frank look.

"Reuben's a fine shepherd," his grandfather had said that morning, "and he can pasture the sheep by himself now it's such good weather."

And so the other shepherds were sitting at home resting.

Reuben stood high up at the top of a hill looking out over the country.

"Oh I do long for him!" he cried to the scurrying clouds. "For the Prince of Peace of the House of David. For the Good Shepherd, who shall be a shepherd to all mankind. Can you who fly so high above the earth not tell me where he is?"

The clouds did not answer. But when Reuben was a little boy he had been given a two-week old lamb. Of course the lamb was now an old sheep, but she was still his favourite animal. The old sheep now butted him in the back of his knees and brushed against him saying, "Reuben, he's on his way here. Didn't you hear the birds telling about it at dawn this morning? They said he was now in Bethlehem in the old stable."

But Reuben did not understand what the sheep was saying. He only thought she was bleating in rather a peculiar fashion.

"Yes, yes," he said, stroking her. "I see you want to comfort me, but how can you do that?"

"If only you understood what I'm saying, you *would* be comforted," thought the sheep.

But Reuben sighed. Then he caught sight of some wayfarers coming along a little path.

144

"Who can they be?" he thought, "A donkey with a big load, a man and a woman. And a boy running in front of them — it can't be . . . !"

He shouted for joy. "It's Mary's little donkey. No other donkey in all the world holds his head like that. And he's trotting along as neatly as ever although it looks as if he's getting old and a bit stiff in the legs."

Reuben rushed down the hill and ran to meet them. And sure enough it was Joseph and Mary! But could that boy, who looked so fresh and lively, be the same sweet baby of the crib?"

Reuben halted. The boy smiled and held out his hand. A fine butterfly had settled on his forefinger.

"Look," he said merrily.

Then Reuben recognized the shine in his eyes. It *was* Mary's child, the little child for whom the angels had sung.

And Reuben jumped high into the air with gladness and shouted with joy. But all the sheep gathered round the donkey to hear how he had led Joseph and Mary to safety in Egypt.

"You are such a capable donkey," they said, "the best in the whole world."

"I didn't manage it all by myself," said the donkey. "At first I was helped by the good angel, and then also by the big camels."

"We've always heard that camels are proud beasts," said the sheep.

"Oh no, they're very kind and clever."

Reuben brought the travellers home with him to the shepherds. Then there was great rejoicing. They got up a great feast and many shepherds from other parts came to see the child about whom their comrades had told so much. The old shepherds told them again and again how it was on the night when they heard the angels' song and how they had gone to Bethlehem and found the child in the manger.

But the little one did not want just to sit still and be admired. He helped Reuben to look after the donkey and to shut the sheep in their pens for the night.

He was strong now, and he had never been faint-hearted. When the big billy-goat came and shook his huge horns right in front of him, he just laughed and patted the billy-goat's nose. The goat felt rather ashamed and became quite tame.

And the boy enjoyed watching Reuben look after the sheep and hearing him tell how to find the best wells and the greenest grass.

"I'm going to be a shepherd when I grow up," the child explained. "A good shepherd who is always on the look-out in case his sheep start straying."

"You shall be the Good Shepherd of all mankind," said Reuben, "And I will follow you wherever you go."

The little one took Reuben by the hand.

"Do you really mean that?" he asked eagerly.

"Yes I really do mean it," said Reuben. "I decided on that when I saw you in the manger."

"Oh that is good of you!" said the boy. "You and I will go shepherding together."

Up on a cliff three men stood on the look-out.

"There are some travellers over there," said the eldest. "Shall we rob them?"

"No," said the two others.

"But we could get some money to buy better tools," he said persuasively. "We should find it easier to get work."

"If we start robbing now, we shall never be able to stop again," objected one of the others. "We'd better not try."

"Oh, if only I could talk to good Mary," sighed the second one to himself, "I should be able to bear hunger and thirst a little better."

146

"Look," said the older man, "it's only two people and their donkey has a mighty big load."

"You can't tell what's in it at this distance," objected the youngest.

"We can go half-way towards them anyway," said the eldest. "We can hide behind those rocks and easily attack them when they come out of the ravine. But if they seem to be poor, we just stay where we are and let them go on. They won't see us."

The others were unwilling but they went along to wait behind the big rocks. The eldest said: "I'll take on the first one that comes if he looks as if he has anything worth taking, and then you take on the second. We don't need to hit them so hard that they would be badly hurt. Then we'll take the donkey and his load and make off."

So there all three of them stood waiting.

"That's odd," thought the first, "It smells like fresh spring flowers, like in our hut that night when Joseph and Mary were there. Can the scent really come all the way here from the fields of Bethlehem?"

"Strange," thought the second. "What a lot of birds there are! I haven't heard the birds singing like this since the birds of Nazareth sang for us."

But the third one had already heard footsteps. He gripped his cudgel and got ready to attack, when a little boy shot forward out of the narrow defile.

The man was so surprised that he stood still with his cudgel raised. The child turned and caught sight of him. He called out a cheerful greeting and held out a loaf of bread which he was carrying.

The man dropped his club, but before he could make up his mind to take the loaf the child had placed it in his hand. Then the child ran back and said something to his parents.

"Good gracious Joseph", cried the woman, "if it isn't the good men from the hut in the mountains!"

She stepped forward and held out her hand to the three men.

"Oh how happy I am to see you again," she smiled. "I have often thought of you."

"Mary," all three of them cried together, "is it really you?"

Then they were all talking at once, Joseph and Mary and the three men. The boy had got hold of the robber's cudgel and was using it as a hobby-horse.

"How have you been getting on?" asked Joseph.

"Badly sometimes, little better at other times," said the oldest. "We've not had much luck with getting work for a long time now."

"It's been a long time since we could eat our fill," said the youngest.

"You shall eat with us today," said Mary. "Now look, sit down here and we'll rest for a bit."

Joseph brought out food from the baggage.

"Work," he said. "In Bethlehem I met a man who needed men in his vineyard. Go there and you'll get. . ."

"No one will take us on," interrupted the youngest gloomily, "for we need some better tools."

Mary looked at Joseph, who nodded and took out his purse.

"Here you are," he said and offered the young men a gold coin. "That will do for tools for all three of you."

"But we can't take your money," protested the eldest. "You need it yourselves."

"I got it from a good merchant, and a gift brings greater joy if it can be given further," said Joseph, laying the coin in the man's hand.

"Didn't I know that everything would be better and easier as soon as you came!" exclaimed the man. "And that you should come just today! For to tell the truth we had almost turned to robbery again."

148

"Wonderful are the ways of God," said Joseph.

"And this is your boy," said the youngest. "Fancy him being so big already! What's his name?"

"My name is Jesus," said the boy readily. "It means 'helper'."

"Just so," the man smiled "and who are you going to help?"

"Everyone!" said the boy.

"I believe you will," said the man, "if you grow to be like your parents. I never met anyone who has helped me as much as they have done."

Some days later the travellers reached the little village where they had stopped the first night.

"Now we'll soon be home," said Mary. "Won't that be wonderful. Think how many years have gone by. And you my child, you've never seen your home! But soon you'll be able to enter its doors, and meet all the animals."

"All the sheep and the goats and the lambs and the kids," asked the boy, "are they my animals too mother?"

"Yes, they're yours too, We'll have them together you and I."

"May I take them out to graze? And give them food and water?"

"You can come with me every day and do that," promised Mary. "But you shall also help father, and learn to plane and saw and use a chisel."

The boy began to dance along the road in front of the donkey. And the worn-out animal thought of the lovely meadows in Nazareth and of his friends waiting at home there, and he gave out a little joyful whinny.

"There's a village behind the hills," said Joseph. "We'll seek a night's lodging there for we won't reach home tonight."

149

Suddenly the donkey started to move quickly because he badly wanted to get in and rest.

Joseph lifted the boy up and carried him on his arm while the sun began to go down. The child fell asleep at once with his head on his father's shoulder.

When they came to the village street Joseph stood hesitating, but the donkey trotted on.

"See," said Mary, "the donkey knows where to go. It's a long time since he's done that. Perhaps he's seen the angel again."

But the donkey had only recognized a voice again, a very good friend's voice. He had heard the active little boy who had once promised to gather hay for him. The donkey had heard him shouting in the distance. Now the boy caught sight of the donkey. He rushed towards him and flung himself on his neck.

"They're coming, they're coming!" he called.

Then Mary recognized the boy and his sisters.

"O Joseph, how clever our little donkey is. He remembered that we promised to visit these people on our way home, and we'd forgotten. Lucky he saved us from breaking our promise."

So they went with the boy to his home. The big sister was allowed to carry the sleeping child, but the smart boy led the donkey into the steading and helped Joseph to unload. Then he opened the trap-door of a little hay-loft and showed all the good hay. Joseph was amazed. He never dreamed that a boy would keep his word so well.

In the poor household there was great joy when the unexpected guests came. The mother had not very much to offer, but Mary brought out honey-cake and other good things which she had received from the merchant. The children had never known such a feast.

"The richest farmer in the place held a feast yesterday, but we weren't invited," said a little one, "but now we've got a much finer feast than anyone else."

Yes, brother and sisters thought so too.

The big sister undressed Mary's sleeping child, washed him and laid him in bed, while the others watched. "Isn't he lovely!" she said.

"Oh yes," said all the little ones, "What's his name?"

"His name is Jesus," replied Joseph.

The next morning the children were allowed to accompany the wayfarers for some of the way, just as they had done the time before.

"What shall we do with all the hay?" enquired the bright lad. "the donkey has only eaten a little little bit. Can you take it in sacks for him?"

No, Joseph could not do that, and anyway the donkey was too heavily laden already.

"But what shall I do with all the hay, as we haven't got a donkey?" said the boy, troubled. "I have told father so many times he ought to buy one but he doesn't seem to want to."

"No, because he can't afford it," said his big sister. "You shouldn't go on pestering him."

"But it would be so nice to have a donkey," said the boy. "He and I could work in the vineyard and earn so much money! But no one will lend us money for a donkey, even though I would pay it back later."

"I'm sure you would," said Joseph, "and so I'll lend you a gold piece."

The boy could not believe his ears.

"Are you rich?" he asked, "We all thought you were poor."

"Indeed we are poor," said Mary, "but we poor people must help each other, and now that Joseph has got some money from a rich merchant he passes the gifts on."

It is impossible to describe how happy the children were! They laughed and shouted with joy, and jumped about, but happiest was Mary's child. He clapped his hands when the boy with the gold piece in his hand turned somersaults on the ground in front of Joseph.

In the afternoon the travellers had still a good way to go to Nazareth. It had been a hard day, and Joseph thought that they should stay with someone they knew in a neighbouring village and do the last bit of the way the next day. He was tired, Mary was tired and the donkey was hardly able to take a step. The only one who did not show any signs of tiredness was the child Jesus, who ran cheerfully beside the donkey, chatting away.

Even so the exhausted animal refused to stop. He just went on and on, although Joseph shouted that they should rest.

"Joseph, what's wrong with the little donkey?" asked Mary surprised.

"He can't be seeing the angel now," said Joseph. "There's no danger here. And we know the way exactly. Stop now, little friend."

But the donkey did not stop and the boy kept on with him. The two understood each other so well.

"Do you think the donkey's seen an angel?" Mary asked the little one.

"I have just seen an angel myself," said the boy, "he beckoned for us to hurry. I told the donkey and he started to hurry."

"Then we'd better just keep on going till we get home," said Joseph.

"Of course," said Mary. "Just let's keep thinking we'll soon be home."

"Home it is," said Joseph, hitching his load higher on his back.

In Nazareth

That very afternoon the rich potter came to Mary's sister and her husband and said:

"I will buy Joseph's house and piece of land today. I must start with my new building."

"Not yet," cried Mary's sister. "Wait till autumn."

"By autumn my new pottery must be ready," said the potter. The husband agreed and so they both went out to have a look at the little house belonging to Joseph and Mary.

"The trees will have to go!" said the potter. "I'll send a man to chop them down tomorrow."

"But the animals?"

"Slaughter the old ones, then sell the young ones to the cattle-dealer. He's just getting ready to go to market tomorrow. So you'll have to sell them this evening."

So the two went off to clinch the bargain.

And what alarm there was in the little steading! The sheep bleated in despair, the goats butted with their horns and stamped with their hooves trying to get through the fence. And all Mary's birds! Were all the trees to be felled where they had their nests? What a disaster was going to overtake them all!

"Won't Mary come home? Is there no sign of the donkey away over there in the hills?"

The birds flew off to have a look.

"Any sign of them?" called the sheep.

"Can you see them at all?" cried the goats.

"There *are* some wayfarers coming, but they're still far away," said the birds, "and they've got a donkey."

"It must be them," said the sheep.

"Who else could it be?" said the goats.

The birds flew off to meet the approaching wayfarers.

And sure enough it *was* Joseph and Mary and the donkey! But who was the lively little boy leading the donkey by the bridle? And *where* was the little baby that Mary had given birth to in Bethlehem? The birds were very disappointed.

"Oh how stupid you are!" said a clever dove. "Don't you realize that the baby has grown so big because they've been away for so long?"

"Yes of course!"

The song of joy that now rose to heaven called to all the other birds in Nazareth and they came flying at once and joined in.

Joseph lifted the boy on to the donkey's back.

"You shall ride into Nazareth," he said.

The boy gave a shout, the donkey arched his neck and tripped along as lightly as in his youth. Mary and Joseph laughed and the birds trilled with all their might.

And so they made their entry into Nazareth.

"What's this?" wondered the people and ran out to see. "Who are those coming in the light of the setting sun? See how it is shining around them. Have they come from paradise? And that singing of the birds, what does it mean? Or is it angels who are singing?"

"No, it can't be angels," said others, "It's only a boy laughing and shouting. But who are they?" They soon saw that it was Joseph and Mary. The neighbours went out to meet them.

Mary's sister came out into the street. She was weeping because her husband was just about to sell the house belonging to Mary and Joseph.

154

Then the neighbours called out: "Cheer up! Your sister's here!"

Oh, how happy she was, and her husband too! He thanked God for letting Joseph and Mary come in time so that their house was still there. Of course the potter was annoyed at first, but he soon got over it and said he was glad that no wrong had been done.

"Come in, come in," invited Mary's sister, and lifted the boy off the donkey. "Come in and have something to eat."

"We must first go to our own home," said Mary. "We've been longing for it every day for many years, and the boy must see his home at last."

"But you'll come back won't you?" said her sister. "I can't see enough of your boy. What's his name?"

"My name is Jesus," said the boy. "You can come home with us."

So Mary's sister set him on the donkey again and went with them to Joseph's homestead.

The animals were absolutely quiet when everyone arrived. The birds had already told them the good news and now they stood all packed tightly together trembling with hope.

"Here I am now!" said the little donkey. "It's been a long journey. But look who I've got on my back!"

Oh yes, they saw all right. Joseph lifted the boy off and Mary opened the gate and went in to the animals who pressed round her. They all nudged and butted to be petted.

"My dear, dear animals," said Mary, "did you miss us very much? I've always been thinking of you, you know."

The boy held out his arms to all of them. "Come, all my little lambs," he whispered happily.

And the lambs and the kids came nearer cautiously and sniffed his hands and let themselves be patted.

"Such friendly kind hands he has," they whispered to each other.

"Am I a shepherd now, mother?" he asked, "now that I've got sheep and goats."

"Yes, now you're a shepherd," smiled Mary.

"The Good Shepherd," whispered the sheep and the goats. "Our Shepherd."

And the birds of Nazareth sang:
"The Good Shepherd has come home
Yes, he has come home at last
And God is good."

"Oh how clever and capable you are, little donkey,"

156

said all the animals when the donkey had told them about the long journey. "How good it was that you could see the angel."

"I didn't see him on the way home," said the donkey, "for my eyesight is now rather poor. But it didn't matter because the boy saw him, and then we just had to go where the angel wanted us to. But dear me, I *am* tired now, and my legs are troubling me so badly you wouldn't believe it."

"Well you can rest now, little donkey," said the animals, "you have truly earned it, and we're so glad you're home. How we've missed you! Just imagine, you really are home at last. The child has come home too, and Mary."

"Yes, and Joseph," said the oldest sheep.

"And the cleverest donkey in all the world," piped up a little kid, scampering round with joy.

Christ Legends

Selma Lagerlöf

Selma Lagerlöf weaves the history and geography of the Holy Land into a series of legends which follow apocryphal events from the life of Jesus to the Crusades.

Festivals with Children

Brigitte Barz

Celebrating festivals is an important part of a child's life. The author describes the nature and character of each Christian festival, its symbols and customs, and gives practical suggestions for celebrating these festivals in the family.

Floris Books